FLOORBURNS

More than a good basketball story, "Floorburns" goes behind Friday night's score to find out why Les Beach, the varsity star, acts as he does. Les, a belligerent young athlete from the "wrong" side of town, brings troubles on himself with his short temper, but through the friendship of interested people like Coach Raines and Judy Merrill, he takes some steps toward maturity and changes from a bad actor to a great player.

JOHN F. CARSON

has been hailed by THE CHRISTIAN SCIENCE MONITOR and other journals as one of the best writers of sports stories today. His books stem from first-hand experience with his subject. Principal of a high school in his native Indiana and a former teacher of English and biology, he is continually involved in various extra-curricular activities and is a lover of sports and the outdoors.

LAUREL-LEAF MAYFLOWER BOOKS

are a new series designed especially to entertain and enlighten young people. The finest contemporary mystery, adventure, romance and action novels, as well as exciting non-fiction, form a singular list of books for leisure reading. The series is prepared under the direction of M. Jerry Weiss, Chairman, English Department, Jersey City State College; Charles Reasoner, Associate Professor, Elementary Education, New York University; and Ned E. Hoopes, Instructor, Hunter College High School and Hunter College.

JOHN F. CARSON

FLOORBURNS

WILDSIDE PRESS

CHAPTER ONE

SOMETHING WAS IN THE AIR THAT MORN-
ing. The suppressed excitement surged through the
halls of Raisner high school. The undercurrent broke
into the open when the gray-haired basketball coach,
Jim Raines, tacked a piece of paper on the bulletin
board. Almost from nowhere, boys gathered to read
the long-awaited notice.

One boy had to let off steam; his slang expression
voicing the sentiments of the excited comments.

"Hot dawg!"

"Yeah man, basketball practice starts tonight!"
Those fortunate enough to be in choice positions were
pressed from their places as others jostled forward to
read the announcement for themselves.

A rangy, black-haired student stood silently on the
fringe of the group. He was content to stand there
with his hands thrust in his pockets. No one could
have suspected his fingernails were biting into his
palms, because his face was expressionless.

"Say, I wonder—" one towhead said.

"Wonder if you'll make the team, Sandy? You're always wondering about something," someone laughed.

"Well, sure, about that, but I was thinking about
Les Beach."

The group fell silent. The tall youth at the back of
the group felt his face tighten. He felt an impulse to
say something. Instead, his eyes flashed with a hard
brightness.

"Yeah, I know what you're thinking. The big cheese himself."

"And how! Boy, it's a wonder Raines put up with Beach as long as he did. Did you ever see such a cocky guy as Beach?"

"Boy, he thought he was the whole team! I guess Raines changed his tune."

"You don't think the guy would have enough brass to come out for the team this season, do you?"

"I know I wouldn't if I were in his shoes," a boy laughed without humor. A few others chimed in.

"It would sure take nerve."

"Don't ever get the idea Les Beach doesn't have the nerve. Still, I don't know. Fur really flew when he and Raines had that showdown, or so I've heard."

"I never did understand what really happened when Beach was booted from the team," a boy admitted. A few shrugged their shoulders.

"I guess no one really knows much about it. Most of the fellows who did know much about it were awful quiet. Anyway, they graduated last June."

"Say, that's right! All of the starting positions of the varsity are wide open!"

The optimistic chatter spurted out again as each boy gave tongue to that idea. Of course, they had all known chances were better this year for lower classmen, but it sounded good, and they liked to talk about it.

"Wouldn't it be a joke if old Les found himself playing on the reserves this year! Boy would that fry him," someone exclaimed.

"You got to admit Les can play basketball."

"I don't think we'll have to worry about him," someone volunteered.

"I don't know about that. Les may be a coach's nightmare, but he's plenty tough, and you know it."

"Nuts. Why didn't the old man string along with him, then?" Jake Koons wanted to know.

"Me, I'm going to let you worry about that one, Jake. I don't play guard. You do. And so does Les."

"Whatsa matter, Rog, you chicken?" Jake said.

A few of the boys in the rear of the group looked uneasy. Only now had they realized that the much-discussed Les Beach was standing at their elbows. Their faces slid away from those eyes in embarrassment. They shuffled to get out of his way.

Les looked at the bulletin board and turned around to face the group. His face was bitter. Jake Koons had been the last speaker, so he addressed his remark to him.

"Get out of my way!"

A strained silence fell over the group. Someone coughed nervously. Jake seemed to measure Beach, then he stepped aside. Les pushed carelessly past him and went down the corridor.

"Whew! Big, isn't he?"

"Big and mean."

"Who does he think he is, ordering us around?" Jake's eyes were resentful.

Roger Larking faced Koons.

"Who's chicken now?"

"What did you expect me to do right out here in front of the principal's office? Use your head for once. That guy's day is coming!" Jake snorted in real or pretended disgust and left to go to his first hour class. He walked alone.

"What do you think, Rip? Think Les will come out for basketball?"

"So what if he does? Anyway, I don't think he will. He's a strange guy. Sits across from me in the biology lab, you know. Never says a word to anyone. Just glares at everybody and everything. He's got a chip on his shoulder, and I wouldn't want to be the one to try to knock it off."

Rip Castner was highly regarded by his friends, and they were glad he had been honest enough to say what most of them had been thinking.

"What a rat race it will be if Beach does come out for the team."

"Jake Koons knows better than to tangle with Les, is all I can say."

"It all adds up to an interesting season. See you at practice."

In spite of algebraic equations, Caesar's wars, gerunds and participles, and distinguishing the legislative, executive and judiciary branches of the government, the school day did end. Thirty boys dashed to the gymnasium. Locker doors banged open.

"Last one on the floor is a monkey," Rip called back over his shoulder as he dashed up the steps two at a time. Others thundered on his heels.

Basketballs were snatched up by the lucky leaders. The gym became filled by the familiar sounds of boys' voices, arching shots and the bouncing of basketballs on the hard maple strips.

Jake Koons took a ball off the backboard and dribbled out to the center of the floor with it. He nudged Roger Larking, who was standing beside him.

"Looks like Beach isn't going to show."

"I hadn't noticed, but I guess you're right." Rog caught a pass from Rip Castner.

"Guys like him never show when the chips are down," Jake said. His satisfaction was obvious.

CHAPTER TWO

LES HAD BEEN WATCHING THE GIRL ALL through the last hour geometry period. Judy Merrill. She was the recent transfer student from Summerville. When the class bell rang, he managed to be walking beside her when she stepped into the hall.

"Oh, hello," the girl said. Les could detect nothing in her tone. She didn't act pleased, but she didn't act like she wasn't, either.

"Mind if I walk to your locker with you?" Les said. He felt awkward. He hadn't learned much about girls. He had been too interested in sports.

"Won't you be late for basketball practice?" Judy asked. Her eyes looked innocent. You never could tell about girls. Did she know about him? Was she trying to find out something?

"I'm not going out for basketball," Les answered after a pause. He didn't know why he had said it. He really wasn't too sure in his own mind. Now he had committed himself. Well, what was the difference? Old man Raines wouldn't let him last long if he did.

"From all the talk I heard today I thought you were one of the big stars," Judy said. Were her eyes laughing at him? Was she baiting him? He felt the flush in his face and bit his lip to keep from making a retort.

"If you heard anything about me at all, it wasn't good," Les said. He avoided looking at her. Someone bumped against his shoulder and he wanted to reach

out and smack him to relieve his thoughts. But he
didn't. He just kept walking along with his hands
clenched at his sides.

Les leaned against the wall and watched the girl
twirl the combination of her lock while she struggled
to keep her books from slipping from her arms. He
made no effort to help her. Let her help herself, he
thought sullenly. Why was he even here with her? He
should be down at Robbins' supermarket at his job.
She made him feel foolish without saying so. He had
to say something.

"You're from Summerville, aren't you?" It was silly.
Everyone knew Judy Merrill was from Summerville.

"Why, yes, yes I am. Say, I remember you from last
year. Didn't you play guard against us? I mean,
against Summerville? I keep forgetting I no longer go
there to school."

"Part of the time. I rode the splinters the last half.
The coach canned me from the team that night."

"Oh, I didn't know. What happened?"

Les wanted to explode and tell someone about that
night. Its memory was fresh in his mind. Eighteen
points in the first half, and Jim Raines had him kicked
off the team! But he didn't tell her. Why, he didn't
know.

"Nothing. You can hear about it from some of these
other guys. They seem to know more about it than I
do. I'm the fall guy, that's all."

"I'd rather hear it from you, Les." The girl looked
up expectantly.

"Well, you won't, so forget it."

"Maybe I'll be seeing you around." The girl's tone
was cool.

"What are you, a letter sweater chaser?" he exploded. He saw the blue eyes frost and he knew he
had made a mistake. Too late for that now.

"I'm sure you'll never know!" Judy snapped. She
tossed her blond hair, and without further words she

turned away from him. He stood there and watched
her walk down the deserted school corridor. He
jammed his hands in his pockets and walked in the
opposite direction.

Past the library, around the corner, now he felt the
muscles tighten in his stomach. The double doors of
the gym stared back at him. He could hear the boys
yelling inside, catch a glimpse of a ball going through
the air, and he caught himself straining forward. He
so much wanted to be inside! Once more he felt
moved to make a decision, a different one this time.
Then he sneered at his own weakness. He shrugged
his shoulders and walked past the gym doors without
taking a second look inside.

So this was the end of his basketball career! All the
years from junior high school on were dumped just
like that. He snapped his fingers without knowing he
did. Yeah, and that sob sister Raines had picked him
up in junior high and told him he would make a great
basketball player someday. Well, that day would never come. The old man had dumped him, used him for
an example in some crazy moral lesson. So he had broken training a few times. Other guys did. He still gave
out plenty in practice, yeah, in games too. But Raines
was one of those strait-laced guys who wanted you to
do everything like out of books. But who had scored
the points when they were needed? Who had broken
up the defense? Who had taken the rebounds off the
boards? Yeah, who had done all the dirty work while
those other guys had stood back waiting for the pass-
out? Les Beach, that's who! Why shouldn't he take the
shots if he did all the work? Let them get a few floorburns if they wanted to be heroes! But no, Raines had
called him a ball hog, and, yeah, what were some of
those other remarks, as if he would ever forget them!
"Self-centered, conceited, biggity, headline hunter."
The old man had nearly blown a gasket. He wished he
had.

Five years of backslapping, two varsity letters, one in his freshman year and the other in his sophomore year, and the old man had given him the boot. Character building, he called it. Hah! Raines hadn't won any more games without him, had he? Heck, the team got shellacked in the first game of the sectional by little Finley. When a coach got the socks knocked off of him he could always scream he was a character builder. It sounded good, but it didn't win any ball games!

CHAPTER THREE

WHILE JIM RAINES STRUGGLED TO IRON out his early season difficulties in the gymnasium, Les was trying to adjust to school routine without basketball. He knew what he was up against, having faced a similar situation last year after being unexpectedly dropped from the varsity at mid-season. Never a social mixer, he could foresee a long winter of classes and his after-school job down at Robbins' grocery.

He steered a wide path around the gym doors. He didn't trust himself to look inside at the big hardwood court with the brightly-polished floor.

In biology class, he was often tempted to ask Rip Castner, his lab partner, how practice was coming along. He knew Castner was trying out for center on the team. Les stifled the idea and turned his attention to his work. Frequently a good student, Les's grades were getting better. But they should be, he didn't have anything else to do. When he cracked Mr. Harbison's pet biology examination with a 99, the teacher began to take an interest in him.

At first Les was slow to respond to kind attention. He wasn't used to people making friendly overtures to him. For a few days it almost made him forget basketball, but not quite.

At night Les would lie in bed and stare up into the darkness. He could imagine he heard a basketball bounding softly. Sometimes it would almost seem to be in the room with him. When that happened, he would sit bolt upright in bed and stare out the window. If the stars were out, he could see Hilton's house through the trees. There was usually a light on in the back bedroom because of Billy. It seemed as though Billy had been ill a long time. At least, he couldn't remember when he had seen the kid last. He really should go over and ask about Billy sometime.

There were other things to think about. Les often tried to recall what his mother looked like. All he could remember, try as he might, was a thin, worn face that stared unseeingly at him. That had been a long time ago.

He put his arms behind his head and brooded.

Then there was his father. People said he was no good. They would look at the skinny, black-haired kid that had been him and then point an accusing finger at Sam Beach and say he wasn't a fit father for such a small boy. But no one offered to help. He remembered that part of it with a particular bitterness. He had been too young to know where his father had been going at night after sending him to bed. But it wasn't long before he awakened in fright to hear his father stumbling and lurching through the dark house. His dad would yell at him to go to sleep, but he couldn't. After a while, his father would come to his bedside and ask to be forgiven. He never said what he wanted to be forgiven for. Maybe it eased his conscience, because he would sprawl fully dressed across the bed and fall asleep.

Les couldn't remember when his father had given up drinking. Maybe the remarks people made about his shiftlessness and unconcern for his boy began to take effect. Most likely it was after the night he had almost been killed at the railroad crossing when he had passed out on the rails. Since then, he had been good to Les. But he hadn't begun to work any more regularly. Once in a while Les would play hooky from school and go fishing with his dad on Cane Creek.

They'd buy a loaf of bread, a dime's worth of baloney at Robbins' and some makings for his dad's cigarettes, and be gone all day.

No boy's dad ever taught him more about the surrounding forested hills, or how to find the best fishing holes among the twisting banks of Cane Creek, or how to identify and track game animals in the snow. He could still see Dad squatting down in the snow, his half-smoked cigarette sticking to his lips, while he explained what animal had passed and how long since it had passed. Dad's way was even more interesting than the way Mr. Harbison taught biology. He could not only remember the things his dad told him, he could actually use them.

Les often felt a streak of disloyalty toward his father when he thought about basketball. If his dad were only holding down a steady job he could go out for basketball instead of working in the afternoon. Well, it wasn't his dad's fault because he wasn't out for the team. Raines probably wouldn't let him come out if he tried.

It was funny about Raines. Sometimes Les had felt closer to him than he had to his own father, especially when he was in junior high basketball. Although the varsity coach didn't have anything to do with junior high ball, he had stayed to watch a game one night after the varsity knocked off practice. That was when the gray-haired coach had begun to give him special attention. He'd slipped him vitamin pills, patted his head and told him they were free samples some salesman had given him. But he reminded him to take them, eat good wholesome food and get plenty of rest.

Why, Les laughed to himself, he had even gone home and drawn pencil marks on the door casing to measure his height, hoping to grow big enough to make a real basketball player. Some of those smeared marks were still there.

But those days had changed. Raines had said he got

too big for his britches, but that didn't explain it. He'd
made the varsity in his freshman year, an unusual oc-
currence at Raisner High School. It took a pretty good
player to make the varsity in his freshman year. He
had received a letter, and for a while he had enjoyed a
burst of popularity. But it hadn't lasted, Les frowned
to himself. He seemed to rub people the wrong way.
Some guys were like that. Even after he had made another letter in his sophomore year, no one changed toward him.

His junior year—that was the explosive one! The
first time Raines had found him in Fred Owens' pool-
room after ten o'clock it wasn't so bad. The second
time, less than a week later, was worse. Incidents
seemed to pile up after that. No one wanted to have
much to do with him at school, and he had tried to get
a little more attention. He'd been kicked out of the
State Theater for disturbing the patrons, as the manager had put it. That got to Raines's ears. He still remembered part of the sermon the coach had preached
to him. Yeah, in the public eye, should be an example,
represented the school, a lot of junk like that.

But he had really found his shooting eye that year.
He could hit. Raines preached to him about that. Holy
cow, how could you satisfy the guy? The other players
that year were a bunch of bums anyway, yet the old
man thought he was going to win a sectional tournament with them. What a pipe dream! He'd been at
that first sectional game, but he was sitting up in the
bleachers. Heck, the team had come closer than that
in the year he was a freshman.

Sometimes, but not very often, he would think
about Judy Merrill. She was the first girl he had
thought he liked. Oh, in those years of freshman ball
some of the upper-class girls had chased after him,
but none of the ones that counted. They reminded
him too much of Shacktown. Judy was different than
those other dizzy-headed girls. She had polish. She

had looks. Heck, she had everything, but she wouldn't
give a guy like him a second look. She was Crosstown.
But then, she just *might* like a guy like him. He had
thought she was a letterman chaser, but in the two
weeks since that blowup he had discovered how
wrong he had been. Although a recent transfer into
Raisner, she had made many friends. Too many
friends. Oh, she spoke to him, but the coolness in her
tone and whole manner had discouraged any further
efforts of acquaintanceship on his part.

As Les brooded about these things he tried to forget
basketball and think about his future. Now he was in
his senior year of high school. Soon he would have to
make a choice of trying to find a way to go to college
or working for someone like Elmer Robbins the rest of
his life. Not that there was anything wrong with working for the grocer, but he wanted more than an average lot in life, to tear himself away from tar-papered
shanties and people looking down their noses at him.
Like being a doctor. There was big money in being a
doctor. Yeah, and people thought you were somebody.
You could have a big car, a nice home and maybe a
cabin up on a lake. He wanted things like that. He'd
decided to be a doctor a long time ago, ever since he
had sat in a waiting room and counted forty people
waiting to see one of the docs in town. Even at two
bucks a clip, that was eighty bucks take for the day.
Not bad. Sure, there were expenses, but the income
was still plenty good.

There were many exciting things he wanted to do,
books he wanted to read; he did read some of them,
but days would slip away between those serious
thoughts. He was mixed up inside. He must have
been, or that wouldn't have happened Saturday morning down at the store.

He had helped Miss Wheeler by carrying her groceries out to her car. Just that, like he had done a
hundred times before. Only this time he had surprised

himself by telling her he would be at church Sunday. Miss Wheeler, he knew, was prominent in church work. She had worked on him enough in the past.

"I think that's grand, Lester." She beamed at him nearsightedly.

He winced when she called him Lester. Of course, that was his right name, but he preferred plain old Les.

"Lester," Miss Wheeler adjusted her glasses to look at him better while she was talking to him, "are you really coming to church tomorrow? Really and truly?"

"Why, yeah, I mean, sure, I'll be there," Les stammered. He was already wishing he hadn't said anything. He didn't know what had made him say it. But he had, and he was stuck.

The following morning, Les felt self-conscious when he entered the kitchen. His dad lowered his coffee mug and gawked at his tie.

"What's the matter with you?" Les said.

"Where you goin', so spiffy like?"

Without answering, Les helped himself from the pan of oatmeal on the stove. He rummaged in the drawer for a spoon while he balanced the bowl in his hand. He straddled a chair across the table from his dad and helped himself to the sugar and canned milk.

"Church," he said finally.

His father leaned back and scratched his whiskers. "Betcha got a girl."

"Bet again." Les wolfed down the cereal. It was getting cold and lumpy.

"I thought the two of us might take a last fishing trip up old Cane Crick before the winter sets in," his dad said. He got up and poured himself another cup of coffee. He waved the pot at Les, but Les shook his head.

"Goin' back into training?" His dad's eyes had taken on a new keenness.

"How can I?"

Sam Beach pulled his chair alongside of his son. His face was lit by a big grin.

"I got news for you, Les boy. Jed Wheeler's takin' me on at the sawmill. I start tomorrow. I'm goin' to hold onto that job, son. Go out for the team again. Shucks, you love that crazy ball game. Remember when we used to go down to the gym together, and I'd wish you luck?" Sam was talking rapidly now. He looked into Les's eyes earnestly. Imploring him. That was the way his dad wanted it. He knew how much he wanted to play.

"Gosh, putting it to me like that, I don't know. I don't know. Raines wouldn't give me a chance. Not after the way we tangled last year. Funny, Bertha Wheeler's the reason I'm going to church today." Les looked startled.

"Then go, Les. But remember what I said about the other. Tell Elmer you can't work during the week. Tell him you're goin' to play basketball!"

"What about Saturdays?"

"That's up to you. You might want a little spending money of your own, you know."

Les stood up. The competitive fires were burning in his eyes. He could feel the pounding of his heart, and he took another breath to steady himself. Why did he feel so weak? Then he began to feel good just thinking about basketball.

"And don't worry about Jim Raines taking you on the squad. He and I had a little talk the other day," his dad said.

"What do you mean by that?" Les asked suspiciously.

"Never you mind. That's between Raines and me. You just go out there and play. Only this year, Les, remember there are four other players on the floor."

"So that's what Raines said, is it?" Les exploded.

"Better get on to church. You'll be late." His father evaded further details with a motion of his hand to-

ward the door. Sam slipped into his coat and picked
up the rusty tackle box. "Me, I'm going fishing." He
winked over his shoulder and pulled the door closed
behind him.

Les stood there, glaring at the door.

"Yeah, he's going fishing!" Then his attention was
arrested by the worn dime on the oilcloth. He stared
at it for a moment, then he slipped it into his pocket
with his own dime, because he knew his dad wanted
it that way.

As he crossed the railroad track at Chestnut Street,
he looked down the rails at the receding figure with
coattails flying and tackle box in hand. Somehow, it
gave Les a contented feeling as he watched.

Fred Owens had already opened his pool hall. Les
was tempted to stop in for a quick game, but he
changed his mind. Fred sat behind the cracked counter like a fat toad. He saw Les and pecked on the window, but Les ignored him. Owens jabbed his cigar
in the air and laughed at him.

The chiming of a church bell reminded Les where
he was going. He walked rapidly toward the sound.

Les nodded at the old maids who smiled at him.
Miss Wheeler squeezed his shoulder as he passed. Mr.
Green, one of the deacons, had given him a handshake
when he came in. The deacons did that to everybody,
not just because it was him, he told himself.

He felt self-conscious in the clothes he wore. He
should have known he'd stick out like a sore thumb
around these other people. His suit coat was bunched
and wrinkled when he unzipped his jacket. He was
glad his coat sleeves could be tugged down far
enough to hide his frayed and unbuttoned shirt cuffs.
His wrists had become too broad for him to button his
sleeves.

Les didn't know where to sit, but finally, as more
people moved up from behind him, he slid into one of
the rear pews. He heard a mother telling her little

boys to stop squirming and sit up nice and tall like the high school boy in front of them. He almost turned around and told the woman he had to sit straight to keep the tight shirt collar from chafing his neck. He didn't, though.

He sang hesitantly, because he didn't know the tune very well. When the notes dipped, he lowered his voice, and when they went up on the lines, he raised his voice.

The congregation was halfway through the second hymn when Les felt, rather than saw, other people coming into the pew. He shuffled awkwardly a few steps so they could all get in.

A delicate perfume drifted into his nostrils. Les fought the temptation to look, but he did. Then his attention was held.

"Good morning, Les," Judy Merrill smiled. Her eyes were warm and friendly.

Les forgot the words. Oh, it was a wonderful Sunday morning!

CHAPTER FOUR

LES WAS BARELY CONSCIOUS OF THE VOCAL solo. His thoughts were churning from the happy coincidence of meeting Judy in church. Was it his imagination or was she warmer and friendlier? She didn't seem displeased sitting beside him. She looked very much as though she shared his pleasure. Well, maybe she did. He wanted to know. When he turned eagerly toward her, however, she smilingly put a finger to her lips and nodded her head toward the pulpit.

Les sank back in happy confusion to listen to the sermon. His neck rubbed against the starched sharpness of the collar as he faced the front. He listened without really hearing what was said. His eyes shifted restlessly from the top of the organ pipes to the flowers on the wicker table in front of the pulpit. Now his gaze swung to the earnest face of Reverend Maynard.

What was that the minister had said? Les alerted himself. Was it a message for him? Les started to spoof the idea. Sometimes a fellow let stained glass windows and organ music make him imagine things. Nevertheless, he leaned forward slightly.

"We are troubled on every side, yet not distressed; we are perplexed, but not in despair; persecuted but not forsaken; cast down, but not destroyed. . . ." The minister rested his hands on the pulpit and looked outward. Les stiffened as their eyes locked for a fleeting moment.

"Do you sometimes feel oppressed, things seem to turn out badly for you, and you keep asking yourself in an inner voice—why me? Do you flare out, or keep it smoldering beneath a hardened exterior? Do things, at times, seem to go wrong when you have tried to do the right things? Or are you misunderstood even by those whom you hold dear? Is everyone seemingly against you?"

Reverend Maynard was looking directly into his eyes, Les thought with a sudden discomfort. The quiet eyes of the minister fastened gently, yet with a compelling command.

"You are not without hope. Regard the key—'but not forsaken'! Are you big enough to face your adversities? Are you big enough to withstand criticism, no matter how misplaced?" The minister's eyebrows raised slightly. Les fought the temptation to nod his head. This stuff was getting him! He purposely diverted his gaze to the piano on the left side of the church auditorium. The voice kept speaking, but Les tried to shut it out. When he did dare a quick look at the pulpit, he saw the minister was speaking to the congregation as a whole. He must have imagined those words had been for him.

Les began to perspire slightly, although the room was not warm. He tried to be unconcerned, to keep the angry wall of bitterness from his heart. But it was still there. He couldn't help it. He was misunderstood, of that he was sure. This stuff was all right for middle-aged people who lived quietly and didn't have much happen to them. There was just enough to it to make a fellow wonder a bit, but that was all. There was always plenty a fellow might think applied to him if you caught him right.

Les mulled over the phrase "persecuted, but not forsaken." It was taken from the Bible, he guessed. He thought about the tar-papered shacks that gave Shacktown its name. He thought of the heavy black smoke from the trains that curled around the houses. He thought of the old newspapers caught by the fences, almost hidden in the tall ragweeds. He thought of his neighbors, rough-shaven and rough-talking, for the most part. Not the Hiltons. No, not the Hiltons. They seemed to have wasted away in their struggle against an illness they couldn't understand. Their faces were haggard with defeat. Maybe it was from staying up too many nights with Billy. The doctor came and went, but Billy didn't seem to get any better.

Why hadn't he gone fishing with his dad? Les brooded. He wouldn't be thinking about all of these things. Enough went wrong without getting more mixed up inside.

The organ music swelled in volume. People were now standing, putting on their coats or moving toward the exits. Les was surprised to see the Merrills were talking to Reverend Maynard in the doorway. When had they gone? He had been so wrapped up in his own thoughts he hadn't known the Merrills had left the pew.

Judy looked back at him strangely, then smiled. He hurriedly put on his jacket and hoped the tear under his arm didn't show.

"Les, you know Reverend Maynard," Judy said. Wasn't that a joke? Here she was almost a newcomer to town, and she had introduced him to his own minister! She had probably seen more of the man than had he, at that.

The deep eyes of the minister seemed to fathom his innermost thoughts. He knows he has me on the ropes, Les told himself. Well, he'd recover. Nevertheless, he was relieved when the Reverend's attention became occupied with other people.

Judy's eyes were lively as she took Les by the arm. "Mother and Dad, I'd like to introduce Les Beach."

Awkwardly Les extended his hand automatically to the man and nodded blankly at Judy's mother.

"Glad to meet you, Mr. Merrill."

"Daddy's a doctor," Judy said quickly.

"Oh, my mistake. Well, glad to meet you anyway."

Les felt the heat from the red glow on his face. He became angry with himself. A heck of an impression he was making on Judy's folks!

"It's our pleasure to meet you, Les." The doctor's smile was pleasant. He looked like a nice guy. There was something about the steadiness of his eyes that gave you confidence. His handshake was firm and sincere. It made a fellow feel better. Maybe that's what made him blurt out, "I'd like to be a doctor someday."

"Fine. The profession always needs more good men."

Judy and her mother were in a whispered conference. Judy whirled around and clapped her hands. Her eyes were shining.

"We'd like to invite you to dinner." Her mother half-encircled her daughter's waist and nodded in agreement.

They're just being polite, Les told himself. Guys like him never got invited anywhere. He was about to refuse, but upon seeing Judy's father nodding agreement as though he had already accepted, he changed his mind.

The four of them went down the church steps together. Les saw some of the fellows on the basketball team staring at him in disbelief. Let them stare, he didn't care. Judy was the best-looking girl in town, and she was with him; or he was with her, he didn't know which. It didn't matter. His spirits lifted.

It was too short a walk, in Les's opinion. He was somewhat surprised when they turned in at the old Spann place.

The Spanns had been old-maid sisters. He used to do odd jobs for them like carrying out the ashes, scrubbing the kitchen floor on Saturdays or putting up the screens in the spring. Sometimes they gave him cookies and a glass of milk with the quarter they usually paid him. They had been nice to him in an impersonal way. He supposed he had been nothing more than a cheap source of labor to them.

Once inside the house, he looked at the familiar high-ceilinged rooms, but the drab wallpaper was now replaced by a brighter design.

"You've kind of livened the place up," Les grinned. He saw Mrs. Merrill was pleased. She moved around birdlike in her home, brushing away dust that wasn't there.

"While Judy and her mother are getting dinner ready, let's go into the study, Les." The doctor was knocking his pipe against the palm of his hand as he walked. Les followed him.

The doctor motioned to a chair. Les sank back into the deep leather seat. He let his breath out slowly. This was the life. Idly he watched the doctor cross the room and place a lighted splinter in the fireplace. The wood began to crackle and the fire soon established itself as a comfortable companion in the small study.

"Like it?" The doctor was grinning at him as he lit his pipe and swung the match several times in the air. For an instant his face was hidden by the swirling blue smoke from the tobacco.

Les nodded and glanced leisurely around the room. He saw several medical volumes on the recessed wall bookshelves, an old-fashioned rolltop desk with papers poking from the pigeonholes and several bronze statues on the mantel. He got up to look at the tiny figures more closely. They were trophies of some kind. He could tell that from across the room. The doctor was watching him keenly as he lifted one in his hand.

"Interested in sports?"

Good grief, Les couldn't help but think, hadn't Judy told her dad he played basketball? Well, he had at one time, he ruefully reminded himself.

"Yeah, I mean, yes, sir, a little." Les held the trophy up to squint at the lettering on its base. The award had been for a half-mile championship. The others, he noticed, were also track championships.

"You did all right for yourself." Les couldn't hide the admiration.

"Not badly, I guess, but then, I was always somewhat disappointed. I wanted to play basketball, but I didn't seem to have the stuff. I've always been quite a basketball fan. Maybe that's why I let Jim Raines talk me into being the team physician this season."

"Yeah, that's right, Doc Olson retired last year." Les spoke before he realized it. Basketball and all that surrounded it underlay most of his thoughts.

"Why aren't you out for basketball, Les? You look like a ball hawk." The doctor studied his build with a quick professional eye.

Les didn't quite succeed in keeping the bitterness from his voice, though he tried.

"I got kicked off the team last season."

"Was there a good reason for it?" the doctor asked, still puffing unexcitedly on his pipe. He didn't put it so a fellow got on the defensive, Les thought. He liked this man. He wanted to be truthful with him. The words seemed to pour from him in his confessional. All the things that had been eating at him from the inside. It made him feel better. His outburst exhausted itself, and he stared moodily into the fire.

"Yeah, there was good reason, plenty of good reason." Les sighed. Was there something about doctors that made people want to tell them all their troubles?

The two of them remained silent for several minutes. Then the doctor winked at him and slapped him on the knee.

"Les, I want to see you out for that team. Your battle will only have begun, but you'll have to make the first move by reporting for practice. Everything isn't suddenly going to turn out all right, but if you stick with it, I think you'll find the answers to a lot of questions you've been asking yourself. You've admitted you weren't a team player. You'll have to become one. It won't be easy. You said you broke about every training rule in the books. You'll have to use will power. What you didn't say, but something I could feel while you were talking, was that you also have a temper. You'll have to learn to control it. I'm not telling you anything you don't already know. Let's go eat."

The doctor poked him good-naturedly to his feet. Les was as tall as Judy's father, and the two of them looked into each other's eyes. Les saw a quiet amusement, a friendliness that strengthened his resolve to go out for that team.

"I think I'll report for practice Monday."

"What is it they say in the books? Oh yes, well, go get 'em, big team, go get 'em! Mother, here we come."

CHAPTER FIVE

LES SLIPPED INTO A BLEACHER SEAT AND pushed the torn brown suede bag out of sight. He rested his face in his hands and silently watched the scrimmage. Unconsciously, his body moved as he watched Roger Larking bring the ball up past the ten-second line. He could almost feel the seams of the ball against his own hands. Les looked into the offensive court, seeking a man to pass the ball to. He grinned wryly to himself and tried to relax in his seat.

Larking faked clumsily with the ball, a fake that fooled no one. The defensive guard made a lucky stab with his hand and hooked the ball away from Larking. In his own excitement, the guard bounced the ball against his foot and it rolled out of bounds. Les winced at the sight of these clumsy executions. He might be better off if he didn't play with this bunch of dubs!

Les glanced across the floor and saw Jim Raines looking in his direction. Raines walked over to his assistant, Tom Williams, and whispered something in his ear. It reminded him why he had come to the gymnasium. It had seemed a comparatively easy decision, yet with the time so close at hand he felt an uneasiness settle over him. He stood up and took a deep breath. He still felt shaky.

As Les walked around the side line he noticed the boys watching him curiously. Let them stare, but it only made him more unsure of himself, almost as though he really didn't belong there. He had just as much right to be there as any of them. Just thinking that put the swagger back in his walk.

The basketballs stopped bouncing as he neared the varsity coach. He was conscious of the silence, the tension, the watchful waiting of the moment. Again he felt that uneasiness, but he was determined not to show it to any of them.

Les stared into the coach's eyes, and there was no friendliness mirrored there. Somehow it steeled him. Just as he thought, they were all against him, especially this man.

"Coach Raines, I want to come out for the basketball team," he said. He was somewhat surprised to hear the harshness of his voice.

Raines snapped his fingers.

"Just like that, huh? Lay around for two or three weeks and then sail out to take over!"

Les felt the surge of anger stifling in his throat. He wanted to hit the coach. No one could talk to him like that! He took a step forward. He heard someone catch his breath behind him. It slowed him down. This was his last chance to play in high school basketball. He couldn't pitch it out the window. There would be no amends, no second chances. He tried to keep his voice even when he spoke.

"I know I've made mistakes. I want to play ball."

It was strictly up to the coach now. Again there was a blanket of silence. Players shifted uncomfortably. Someone bounced a basketball to relieve his feelings as the tension mounted.

"When you play on this team you play as I tell you to play or it's no go. You understand that, Beach?"

"I understand that." He hoped he masked his seething anger.

"These boys have earned their positions. You'll practice with the second string." Raines waited for Les to nod his head and then said, "After that, it's up to you."

Les flushed, but he swallowed both his pride and his temper. He knew he could play circles around any player on the floor. He suspected Raines knew it also. He recognized the challenge. It was strictly up to him now. The coach had given him his chance if he wanted to take it.

"When can I start?" Les asked and bent down to pick up his suede bag.

"Right now, if you can furnish your own practice uniform. Ralph Watts, the student manager, will issue shoes to you." The coach seemed to notice the strange silence for the first time. He motioned to the boys to get on with practice as Les went down the dressing room tunnel.

Ralph Watts looked surprised when he leaned over the half-door into the equipment room.

"You coming out, Les?"

"Raines said to get my shoes from you."

Les frowned when Ralph handed the beaten-up shoes to him. He thrust them back angrily.

"Say, what is this! I used to get new shoes to play in."

Watts cleared his throat.

"Those were the old days, Les. This year Raines says everybody earns what he gets. Anyway, this is all I have left."

"You better mark it down in your book to order a new pair, size ten," Les said. He strode into the locker room and glanced around for an open locker. He found one farthest away from the showers. As he began to undress, however, the old excitement of the locker room smells roused him into speedy action. He almost ripped the buttons from his shirt as he took it off to throw into the locker. He lost little time in putting on his faded uniform. The number eleven which had been his in both practice and games was barely discernible.

The shoes plopped against the concrete as he raced

up the ramp. The baggy sweatshirt, too short at the waist from countless washings, rode high on his chest. Les swung his arms and felt the animal exuberance of good health.

Jim Raines had been watching for him, because he crooked his finger in his direction. He took a seat on the bench and patted it. Les sat down. He was totally unprepared for the kindness on the coach's face.

"It's good to have you back, Les," the man said simply.

"It's good to be back."

The two of them shifted their eyes and looked away for a moment, each busy with his own thoughts. Behind them, Les heard Tom Williams say softly, "The old coach and his protégé."

It did something to Les he couldn't understand. For a moment, at least, he recaptured that warmth for this gray-haired old man who had tucked him under his wings several years ago. Once more they were reunited. It did feel good. He started when he realized Raines was talking to him.

"Les, I'm looking for you to furnish leadership to these boys. They lack game experience. They'll look to you as an example. What kind of an example you set will largely determine how far they will go. A few minutes ago I was resolved to turn you down, but it took guts to come as far as you did, Les, and I admired you for it. You took more from me in two minutes than you would ever have taken last year. You were boiling, and I knew it. If you hadn't checked yourself, Les, you would have been done. You know that, don't you?"

Les nodded his head and looked down at the floor. What was there about Jim Raines that got under his hide when he was around him? Now, he wanted to play for him.

"Les, I want to win a sectional this year. It's my last chance. I retire in June. I've never won one, you know. Maybe this isn't the team that can get the job done. They're young and inexperienced. You're going to be my playmaker. A lot depends on you, Les. These kids need some competition, more than they have been giving each other. I think you're the answer."

Raines got to his feet and motioned him out on the floor. The coach blew his whistle. The boys gathered in a loose circle, eying Beach with puzzlement. Les stared steadily back at them.

"We'll take five more minutes of scrimmage. Dawes, you sit down. Beach, take off your shirt and take his place. All right, the varsity get in the defensive court. Skins, take the ball out at the ten-second line."

Les took the pass-in from Hendrickson and bounced the ball while crouched in place. Ryan moved in too closely and Les faked with his body to the left and cut around him easily. Already he was in position for a clear shot, but somehow he refused the temptation and passed off to Johnny Kerr. Kerr drove in, but Castner blocked his shot.

The skins took the ball from outside. Again Les got the ball and passed off. This time Hendrickson attempted a one-handed push shot from the top of the keyhole. Castner went up for the ball, but Beach had already snatched it from the boards and was out with it. Les turned and dropped a left-hander into the hoop.

The varsity players exchanged quick glances. The action had been fast and they were caught flat-footed. Jake Koons scowled.

"Let me take him," he said to Ryan. The skins were back out at the center stripe and Koons shifted to cover Beach.

Les saw Koons was going to try to take the ball away from him. He saw it in the determined look in his eyes. It was the kind of look that telegraphed, "I'm going to make a monkey out of you. I think

you're overrated!" Les grinned and kept his head up,
although his body hovered closely over the ball.
Koons lunged for him, then, realizing Les was getting
away from him, he turned wildly but lost his balance
and fell to the floor.

Two players converged on Les from the front, but
he back-pedaled and eluded them. Koons had leaped
up and was chasing Les from behind, fouling repeat-
edly, but was unable to capture the ball. Les circled
back out to the ten-second line, letting them crowd
him until they were too close, then, like a shot released, he changed hands and drove around them.
Castner and Joe Taylor went up together in an effort
to stop him, but he delayed a scoop shot and snaked it
through the opening left by their off-balanced positions.

The varsity players looked sheepish. Les pretended
not to notice the fearful looks they cast in his direction. He'd make them hump!

Again and again Les executed those tricky ball-han-
dling capers that left the defense off balance. He especially enjoyed sucking them in and then calmly passing out to someone like Joe Taylor who was standing
unmolested in the clear.

The second team players began to catch the spirit
of showing up the varsity and they began to enjoy
practice. They watched Les for an eye flick, a nod of
the head, passes that cut cleanly through the defense
to bounce but a step ahead of them on their way up to
the hoop.

The coach watched with compressed lips. Les saw
him motion to varsity players where to set up defensive positions, but he eluded the traps. Raines
called a time-out and talked earnestly to the first-
stringers for several minutes. He indicated plays on
the floor with a blunt forefinger.

In the meanwhile, the second-stringers had gathered around Les for their instructions.

When play was resumed, the varsity had gimlet eyes. But Les saw to it that he controlled the ball most of the time and their efforts to get it away from him were fruitless. Time and time again he managed to unbalance the court, and a skin went under for a lay-up. They didn't always score, but Les was getting the majority of the rebounds.

Raines blasted angrily on the whistle to call a halt to the practice, and Les felt relief. He wasn't basketball-hardened yet, and he'd had enough for one night. The second-stringers were sent to the showers while Raines had another session with the varsity.

Les had showered and dressed when he overheard Raines's words as he was coming up the tunnel.

"You got a taste of basketball with Beach out there. He's one of the toughest in the state. Watch the way he works the ball, he's deceptive, the way he takes position under the backboard for those rebounds. . . ."

Les knew Raines had caught sight of him and had ended whatever else he might have said. His spirits lifted. Raines knew he could play ball. But from the looks the others threw over their shoulders he knew he hadn't made his berth any easier. You couldn't show guys up in practice by making monkeys out of them and then have you preached at them on top of it.

As Les neared the exit he saw Jake Koons slow down. He waited for Koons, who had looked to make sure Raines had disappeared into his own dressing room office.

"You want to say something to me?"

"Aren't you the little hero!"

Jake's face showed his dislike.

"It won't take long to find out."

Les turned his head to slide under Jake's fist and threw a chopping overhand right into the varsity player's face. Jake went down with a dazed expression in his eyes. Les leaned over him.

"Don't try that with me again."

Jake scrambled to his feet, his face livid with anger. "I'll get you for this, Beach. Don't forget it."

Les cocked his fist to smash him again, but he heard the coach's door open and close. It was Tom Williams. The assistant coach noticed their strained attitudes and started forward. Jake Koons backed away from Les and continued around the gymnasium.

Williams put a hand on Les's shoulder.

"Watch it, Les. You're only borrowing trouble."

"I'm not running from it, either," Les said. He left the assistant coach standing there looking after him as he went out the gym door.

CHAPTER SIX

LES FELL IN STEP WITH JUDY AS SHE walked down the hall to her first hour Latin class. He was ill at ease with her as yet and didn't say anything for a moment. What did other guys say to girls to pass the time away?

"Hi, there." Judy looked up into his face with a smile of pleasure. Then she steered him from the stream of teen-age traffic.

"What's the trouble, Les? I thought you had reported to practice and your troubles were over." She waited anxiously for his answer.

"Over? Good grief, Judy, my troubles have just begun."

"What do you mean by that?" She shifted her books to her other arm and began to walk slowly. He stopped her with a frown.

"No matter what I do, it turns out wrong. I went out for practice, all right, but some of the guys didn't like the way I showed them up. One of them in particular, Jake Koons. Know him?" Les couldn't keep the anger from showing on his face.

"I know him when I see him, but that's all. Someone said he played on the reserves last year."

"Yeah, he did. If I have anything to do with it, that's where he'll be playing this year, too!"

"Les, what happened? Did you have some kind of a run-in with Jake?"

Les looked at her so darkly that she drew back from him in surprise.

"I smacked him last night, knocked him down." Les knew what Judy would think of something like that. Her blue eyes were wide. She wasn't used to guys like him, he could see.

"You mean you got into a fight? Oh, Les, you have to be careful, this being your last season and all."

He put his hands in his pockets and looked down at the terrazzo floor.

"You don't have to remind me. I know it's my last season, but I'm not taking any of his lip, now, or any other time." He thrust his face toward her.

"Les, you have this all wrong. You can't go around hitting everyone just because you don't like what they say or do. That doesn't solve anything."

"You never lived in Shacktown. A good right is a guy's best friend over there. You fight for everything you get, or you're left holding the sack. First you're a little guy getting knocked around by the bigger guys, then you grow up, then it's your turn."

"Your turn to knock the little guys around? Is that it?"

Les felt the cords in his neck swell, and he had difficulty in keeping his voice steady.

"I never hit anyone smaller than me in my life! Jake Koons is no midget. He jumped me and I let him have it."

A righteousness had crept into his tone.

"Les, promise me something." Judy seemed to poise herself for last second flight into the classroom.

Les was cautious. He knew what she was going to say before she said it.

"What?"

"Don't get into any more fights with anyone on the team."

"What do you want me to do? Stick out my chin and beg someone to pop it? No thanks."

"Just don't do anything that will start a fight."

In that moment Les was more conscious of those blue eyes than he had ever been. They regarded him seriously, but he still managed a certain amount of sarcasm before surrendering.

"That's a small order."

"Promise?"

Her womanlike persistence annoyed him.

"No, I don't promise anything. If those guys think they're going to push me around, they better get some other ideas."

"You don't need to shout at me. When you get rid of that chip on your shoulder, come around and see me sometime," Judy flashed in a show of temper. She moved away and tried to dodge the hand Les put out to detain her when he couldn't think of anything to say.

"Let me alone. I'll be late for class. I should have known you were incurable."

That last remark stunned Les. Was he as hopeless as that?

"Wait a minute, Judy. I'll try."

"Then you do promise?" Judy met his gray eyes with a new look of appraisal.

Les swallowed with difficulty. Few people had ever made him back down, not since Fred Owens had pushed his face in the dirt so hard he could barely breathe. He had been a little guy then.

"Just as you say." He grinned sheepishly.

"Thanks, Les. Things will work out." Judy's hand brushed his arm lightly in assurance.

Les felt a giddiness that was new to him, and he was ashamed at his susceptibility. "I hope so," was all he could manage to say as he backed away. He turned on his heel and ran for his own class before the tardy bell could ring, but he didn't make it. Mr. Keene, his English teacher, silently wrote out a blue slip for him. That meant a detention period for him, but for once

Les couldn't keep a grin from his face. This time it was worth it.

During biology class Rip Castner nodded cordially to him, and Les felt an uplift in spirit. Rip leaned forward on his elbow.

"Say, you really move that ball around," Rip whispered.

Les tried to think of a snappy answer, but an inner bell seemed to ring. This was one of those times he so often rubbed guys the wrong way.

"Thanks." Les was surprised somewhat at his own answer. He saw Rip wink and draw back his head like a turtle retreating within its shell. Mr. Harbison was looming in front of them.

Les met Rip again as the two were entering the gymnasium for practice. They walked together into the locker room. Les envied Rip's free manner. Actions such as these didn't come easily for him. Rip joked with some of the fellows as he threw his books into the locker.

When Les tried experimentally to participate in the light chatter that had sprung up he didn't get much response. A few of the second-stringers like Johnny Kerr did answer, but those guys didn't really count. Well, maybe they did, but somehow he wasn't satisfied. Instead, he felt his temper rising. What did he care for those punks on the varsity? They could take him or leave him. He wasn't going to crawl to them. He set his jaw and finished dressing. He was alone when he went up to the playing floor.

After the boys warmed up Raines began the three-man crossover passes for the fast-break style he hoped to use during the season. The players were required to run at three-quarter speed until one of them got the lay-in shot. That boy was expected to un-notch an extra burst of speed.

In this drill, Les found himself teamed with the least-likely-to-succeed of the varsity. The boys

couldn't handle his passes, and he didn't get a chance
to shoot. He had momentary gratification when the
coach's voice bawled hoarsely a time or two for them
to hang on to those passes.

In fundamental lay-ups, in the conventional ap-
proaches to the basket, Les came into his own. He
could see the others watching him enviously. He was
proud of the steely spring in his legs, and he redou-
bled his efforts in getting up into the air.

Later, in one-court drills, Les could take the ball at
will from the varsity offense. His pressing tactics rattled them, and he kept an accompanying string of
chatter rasping their ears. They weren't used to it, and
they didn't like it.

As the days of practice wore on, Les could feel a
breach widening between himself and the other players. Rip Castner was friendly, but he was about the
only one.

Les could see the boys become angry and dispirited
in turn as he put on the pressure. Although they
played hard, he always made sure he played harder.
Raines began to slip him into Koons's guard spot more
frequently, taking him away from at least one un-
pleasant situation. When he was playing with the first
five, they were relieved from his opposition. As a
guard, and the playmaker, he dominated the ball, and
they became somewhat dependent upon his passes so
they could shoot for the basket.

Time and time again Jake Koons tried to show him
up by attempting to pull a ball steal, but just as frequently Les outmaneuvered him. Raines would frown
at Les from the side lines when he thought he was
going too far in baiting Koons. The coach was well
aware of the animosity between the two guards, and
Les became more cautious in making Jake ridiculous.

On Thursday afternoon before the game, Raines
held light defensive drills. That was the afternoon he
read off the starting lineup against Beucamp.

"Les, go down and take your shower, then stop by my office before you leave. I want to talk to these boys a minute."

Les was puzzled. He knotted the sleeves of his sweatshirt around his neck and got up from the bleacher seat. He couldn't mask the hurt in his eyes. This offhand manner of Raines's could mean only one thing. He wasn't going to start the game. That was it.

As he stripped for his shower, Les no longer had injured feelings. He was boiling angry. He savagely twisted the shower faucet and almost got scalded as he bent down to grope for the handle he had wrenched off. After all his work to make the team. Did Raines still harbor a grudge against him? Come around to his office! Yeah, come around so he could give him another sermon of some kind.

When the team came trooping into the shower room he didn't bother to ask who the starters were to be. He could almost tell by looking at their faces. They looked at him oddly, he thought, but he didn't care. He was getting used to them. He pulled the dressing room door closed against their voices and walked down the passageway to the coach's office. He knocked, and Tom Williams let him in.

"You wanted to see me," Les said. Jim Raines was sitting on his desk top facing the door.

"Sit down, Les, if you can find room. Hey, Tom, clear your duds off the chair."

"What do you want to see me about?" Les waited for an answer. He wanted to get it over with.

Raines hunched forward.

"Les, you've done a good job for me. I wanted you as a playing coach by example, and you've done everything I asked. I like that."

"But I don't start against Beucamp, is that it?"

"Hey, don't look so bitter. Les, I've been watching you. You're learning to get hold of yourself. About the game, being as you wanted to know, I want to find out what these kids can do under pressure. I want to hold you back in reserve, so to speak. If they get rattled, I expect you to straighten out. You have the game experience."

"Sounds like a rosy future for me."

"Maybe you better tell Les what you told the other boys," Tom Williams said.

"Okay, maybe that would help. Les, I told those boys out there a while ago that they were playing with one of the toughest boys in the state. I meant that. I'm not going around tossing bouquets at you until I see what you do for me this season. You've been one of the best, but we don't live on past performances. You play ball for me, Les, and I'll go all the way for you."

Les knew when Jim Raines meant something. He had been associated with this man too many years not to know. Once more that former closeness linked them together.

"You're calling them," Les said.

Les saw the man's face light with excitement and a sudden emotion.

"Les, we just have to get that sectional this year."

So the old man was still daydreaming. Well, maybe he wasn't. Maybe that was the kind of faith he needed as a player.

Les reached behind him and turned the doorknob. He paused a minute before he went out.

"They'll know they've been in a game."

Tom Williams grinned at them as he reached for his T shirt.

"When you two guys stop patting each other on the back, I'll get dressed. It's cold in here."

Les was whistling when he left the gym.

CHAPTER SEVEN

THE GAME HAD ALREADY GONE PAST THE first quarter intermission and the big scoreboard was a grim reminder to the Raisner Tomahawk fans. They were silent. They no longer booed the referees, which at least was comforting to the officials.

Another Beucamp basket made the scoreboard blink again. Les looked up automatically, but he was no longer paying much attention to the game. The bench was crowded and he resented the cramped position in which he was forced to sit. Why wasn't he playing? Wasn't the team far enough behind yet?

Les saw Raines look down the length of the bench, but he avoided looking at him. Some of the guys, he saw, were in the act of peeling their sweatshirts, hoping they were getting their big chance. Surely, there wouldn't be much pressure on them with a score like that. They were here just to play, Les thought. They had already given up hope of winning the game. He gave vent to his disgust by scuffing the toe of his shoe against the hardwood strips of the floor.

"Beach!"

As Les got up from the bench he heard someone behind him groan. He coolly took time to turn around and face the speaker.

"Don't tell me Raines is still carrying that Beach on his team. Of all the self-appointed glory hounds!"

"You talking about me, mister?" Les kept his voice low, but he knew the man had heard him.

"Beach!" Raines grasped him by the arm.

"Okay."

"Go out there and keep possession of that ball long enough for us to score."

Les hopped around as he took off his sweatpants.

"Is that all?" He didn't take into consideration the frayed nerves of a coach who was watching his team get a shellacking.

Instead of answering, the coach pushed him toward the scorekeeper's bench with a hard shove. Again Les heard the man in the reserved seat.

"More of that would do that big-head a lot of good!"

Les was bitterly conscious of the loud chorus of boos when he trotted out to replace Jake Koons. Jake nodded his head backward toward the side line.

"I see your friends remember you from last year."

"Beat it!" Les snapped. He could hear the catcalls and boos like thunder now. He'd show them.

Larry Ryan received the pass-in and dribbled across the center stripe. He stopped too soon when a Beucamp player threw up his arm, faked weakly, and threw a wobbly pass to Les. As soon as Les got possession of the ball he heard some of the loudmouthed spectators chanting from the side lines.

"Shoot! Shoot!"

Les wasn't even in the clear. He bit his lip and passed back to Ryan, the other guard. The ball was returned instantly. It was plain Larry didn't have any plan of attack in mind.

"Shoot! Shoot!" The fans screamed in laughter. He shouldn't be able to hear them, Les kept reminding himself. Was it only in his mind? He barely eluded getting tied up. His face was grim as he passed to Roger Larking who had come out from the corner.

Again the ball was speedily returned. Beucamp players were swarming on Les now. Angrily he tried to dodge them. He could hear spectators shouting in glee as the Beucamp players chased him across the end court.

"Shoot! Shoot!" The mocking chorus was louder now. Others had taken up the derisive shouting.

Les let the pass get away too soon and it bounded high into the reserved section seats. Somewhere, some fans gave a burst of applause, and Les smothered the hot urge to smash someone in the nose. He wiped his wet palms on his trunks as he ran down the floor to get into defensive position. Already he was too late. His man made an easy tally.

The minutes dragged by on the big clock. Les dully wondered when Raines was going to jerk him. He had begun to wish he would. He was furious with himself. He was going to show who with what? Every time he got the ball, the same exasperating chant would well up around him.

"C'mon, hotshot, wake up!" Ryan hissed at him as he started to set up the rotation pattern. Les savagely jerked the ball from Larry's hands. This guy was telling *him* to wake up! Then the ball slipped from his fingers, and almost in a nightmare he watched the number 22 from Beucamp scoop up the ball and take off down the floor.

Clumsily, Les tried to recover. He only succeeded in tripping himself. Awkwardly, he threw out his hands to break his fall. His face was burning in humiliation. From the stomach position he watched number 22 sink another field goal.

When the home-town crowd began to jeer Les struggled to his feet with danger signs gleaming in his eyes. He clenched his fists and headed for the side line and the loudest voices. A barrage of boos almost drowned out the buzzer as Castner signaled the time-out with a frantic T with his hands.

Castner ran up to him and gripped his arm.

"Take it easy, Les!" Les allowed Rip to turn him

around and steer him to the bench. He hunched his
shoulders against the boos and jerked his arm from
Rip's grasp.

Jim Raines met him part-way out on the floor.

"Just what do you think you're doing!" the coach
thrust his face so close that Les could see the gray
bristles on his chin.

"I don't know. I don't know." A wide space opened
for him on the bench, and the boys avoided looking at
him.

"Sit down and cool off!" Raines threw his sweatshirt
at him, and Les caught it with an angry grab. The guy
behind him laughed, but Les didn't give him the satisfaction of turning around to let him bait him further.

What was the matter with him? He knew he could
play better basketball than any of those guys on the
floor. Was he too anxious? What was it his dad had
said on the way down to the gym tonight? Yeah, it'd
be like old times. Wasn't that a laugh? It really was
like old times! Well, he'd had his chance. Les felt like
laughing, crying and fighting all at the same time. Just
look at that Koons gloat!

The gun exploded on a 23 to 9 half-time score. Les
trailed mechanically after the team. He felt strangely
tired and discouraged.

The boys trooped into the dressing room and
slumped against the lockers. Raines closed the door
and leaned heavily on it. He didn't even act as though
he heard Ralph Watts, the student manager, calling
for admission. His face had become ashen. Les took a
quick glance at the coach but lowered his head guiltily as Raines stared back at him.

"You boys are going to have to steady down. You're
not stopping them. We'll put a three in and two out
zone against them to bottle up the backboard. Taylor,
you move out with Ryan. Beach, I want you under the
boards for those rebounds."

Jake Koons jerked up his head sharply.

"Hey, what is this? You mean Beach is going to start this half?"

"Why not?" The coach met his eyes steadily. It was too much for Jake. He jumped to his feet.

"Well, good night, he sure didn't help us any when he did play."

"I didn't see you set the world on fire," the coach answered.

Jake looked at the players around him, but no one let any expression betray what he might be thinking.

"You boys go on up to the floor. I want to talk to Beach a minute." Raines unlocked the door for them to leave. He reached out and slapped them encouragingly on the back as they went out. Koons dodged his hand, but the coach pretended not to notice. He shut the door and faced Beach.

Les saw the strained patience on the coach's face.

"When are you going to conquer that temper of yours and play ball? You acted like any other of these kids, and you have almost three years of varsity experience on most of them."

"You said you were starting me this half. Why, after what I did?" Les stood up with a questioning look on his face.

"Darned if I know. Maybe I got a crazy idea you could be a great ballplayer. Then again, maybe I think someone should knock your block off." The coach grinned crookedly and shook his head.

"Maybe you have faith in a guy that doesn't deserve it," Les said.

"Could be. Maybe I got my dander up when I heard the crowd go against you. Yet I wanted you to take all that because I thought you had it coming to you. Les, you're going to destroy whatever good there is in you if you keep that chip on your shoulder."

"I thought I had control of myself," Les said. He shook his head. Everything he did seemed to backfire.

"All right. You get out there this half and open up on that hoop. Fire whenever you get open."

Les was shaken. This was worse than ever. All the fans were waiting to ride him further. Les felt a kind of nausea sweep over him. When was this persecution going to end?

"You kicked me off the team for that last year," Les said dully. "That bird behind the bench is just waiting for a chance to ride me."

"Are you playing for him, or are you playing for me, Les?" The coach put a kindly hand on his shoulder.

"What do you want me to do?" Les was sharply attentive.

"That's the boy! I know you can hit. We need this ball game to give our kids a boost. They're scared and feeling a little low from the score. Go out there and stoke them up!"

"That's a big order." Les let out his breath slowly.

"I remember a serious-eyed skinny little kid that would have gone out to kill giants for me," Raines said. His voice was soft.

Les grinned at the recollection and felt better. Raines had faith in him in spite of everything. Somehow, the coach understood how things were for him. He gripped the man's hand briefly.

"One giant killer coming up!"

The warning buzzer sounded as Raines and Beach came out to the floor. The boys came in from their warm-up to form a loose circle around them. Jake Koons hung on the outside of the group.

"All right, boys, here it is. Feed the ball to Les this half."

Les saw Koons frown and shake his head. He no longer cared.

Rip Castner looked into the rangy guard's eyes and cracked a big grin when Les winked back at him. The center grabbed his hands and the other players gathered into a tight knot.

"I'm with you, Les boy, let's eat 'em up!" Rip yelled.

Rip's enthusiasm roused a kindred spark. The Tomahawks began to yell excitedly.

A feeble cheer greeted them as they ran out to their playing positions.

The thin-faced Beucamp player, number 22, grinned at Les.

"You coming back for the funeral?" he kidded.

"Yeah, yours," Les flashed. He tensed for the ball to go into play.

CHAPTER EIGHT

LARRY RYAN CAPTURED THE TIP FROM CEN-
ter. He brought the ball down fast, only to stop inde-
cisively as a Beucamp forward made a slash at it
with his hand. A more experienced player than Larry
would have kept going. The ball went back to Beach.

A fan half-stood in his seat as Les came down the
side line. He cupped his hand to his mouth.

"Shoot!"

Les obligingly dropped one in from twenty-five feet
out on the court. Visitors 23, Home 11.

"Hail, the conquering hero!" One rooter jumped to
his feet and waved his box of popcorn grandly in the
air. He frowned quickly as half the box's contents
spilled in a white shower.

Les moved up fast to press the offensive pass-in. His
quick pivot shot was good for two points. Score, Visitors 23, Home 13.

The thin-faced player who had ridden Les but a
few minutes earlier grunted his exasperation as he
again tried to pass in from the side line. He yelled for
help. A teammate came into the back court, but number 22 couldn't get the ball out to him in time.
Raisner's ball!

Rip Castner took the ball outside and tried to hurriedly pass in. However, he was restrained by the referee. Beucamp was able to get set, but Rip got a
bounce pass to Rog Larking in the corner. The forward
was almost trapped before he passed out on the court

to Les who had moved up to relieve him. Les sighted quickly. His one-hander cut the cords cleanly.

"He hasn't changed a bit," one fan growled. Yet, in spite of themselves, other fans who might condemn him tomorrow began to get excited. Only a minute of the third quarter had passed and Les had been responsible for six points!

The big clock had only seconds left of the same third quarter when Les scored his thirteenth point. He had missed but two attempts in his point making spree. He had done the only shooting, as the team had followed Raines's instructions. The score now read, Visitors 23, Home 22.

Fans were on their feet as the Beucamp forward broke loose from the defense and dribbled fast for the end court. Les backpedaled to keep in front of the oncoming player. He was the only obstacle between the Beucamp forward and the basket. He knew the shot would be one of those last second attempts before time in the quarter ran out.

Les went high into the air as the forward flipped the shot on the dead run. His fingers deflected the ball, and in that instant he knew he was going to be hit by the fast-moving player. Just as the student fans had begun to shout, the player, unable to check his speed, collided heavily with the rangy Tomahawk guard. Les crashed heavily to the floor with the Beucamp forward sprawling on top on him. His head rapped against the floor and he was conscious of pain shooting across his temple.

Les stumbled groggily to his feet, staggering to regain his balance. The Beucamp player tried to help him, but he waved him away. Les put his hand to his forehead as Ralph Watts ran up to him, towel in hand. Raines must have called time, Les thought.

"You all right, Les?" Ralph was dabbing the sweat from his face. Les caught a glimpse of a red smear on one corner of the towel. His scalp felt loose to his exploratory touch. He began to walk to the bench, but the referee was now motioning to him from the foul stripe. He was holding the ball in his left hand.

Rip Castner caught up with him as he stood there blankly.

"He wants you to shoot the foul, Les. Can you do it?"

The gym was strangely hushed as Les took the ball from the referee. Fans sitting at the end of the court could see the red matting in his black hair.

Les brushed his hand across his eyes to clear the red haze, steadied himself, and flipped the ball through the hoop for the tying point, 23-23! The buzzer ended the quarter.

As Les walked back to the bench he received the only sincere ovation he had experienced in his basketball career. It sounded good to him. It made it feel worth while to get clobbered like that.

Doctor Merrill got up from the end of the bench, ready with a damp pad to bathe his face.

"Let's go into the dressing room, Les." The doctor took him by the arm and half-led him through the tunnel and down the steps. Inside the locker room, Les slumped down on a bench. He winced as Doctor Merrill put something that stung on the wound.

"You got a nasty bump." The doctor squinted at his scraped forehead and hairline. Les could feel the throbbing of a growing lump under the doctor's light touch.

"Yeeow!"

"Hurts, huh?" Judy's father laughed. Les didn't see much humor to it, but he grinned weakly in response.

"Takes a lot to hurt us Shacktowners," he said.

"Especially on the head!"

Les let that one pass and cocked his head to hear the sounds from the playing floor. His mind was still on the game. He smiled when he heard an especially loud cheer. The locals must have scored. Seconds later, when the cheers broke out in less volume, he guessed the Tomahawks must have regained possession of the ball. The following groan and shriek indicated Raisner had attempted to score, had failed, and had lost possession of the ball.

Les and the doctor looked up as a light, hesitant knock rapped on the door. Judy's father stepped across the room and opened the door a crack, then widened the gap to admit Sam Beach.

"Hi, Dad."

"How are you, son?" Sam bent down to squint at the wound critically.

"I'm okay. Good grief, you'd think I was really butchered!"

His father patted his shoulder. As his father stepped back he saw Doctor Merrill unwinding a strip of gauze.

"Hey, what are you doing?"

The doctor grinned but motioned to him to keep still. Skillfully he applied a neat white crown to Les's head.

Les waited impatiently for him to finish, then pushed to his feet.

"I want to go back up there and play."

"Whoa, take it easy. You've played this one out for the evening."

Les swung around and began to pace the room in agitated strides. He couldn't keep quiet. He had to keep moving. He was keyed up.

With a shrug the doctor picked Les's sweatshirt from the bench and draped it over the boy's shoulders.

"There's nothing to keep you from watching the game, Les."

"But I can't play, is that it?"

"I'd prefer not. We might need you the rest of the season."

Les looked at his father, but Sam's face showed that

he agreed with the doctor. He looked at the two men and then went out the door.

The boys on the bench made room for him. Their "Nice going" made Les feel humble. He whispered a low "Thanks" and sat down. It felt good to hear those remarks. The newly-found happiness made his lips tug in a grin he couldn't keep back. He turned his attention to the game.

The Tomahawks were kindled with new fire. Oh, they hadn't become world beaters, but they were playing over their heads. The score was deadlocked at 36-36.

Jake Koons, who had replaced him, electrified the fans by getting away from his guard to break for the basket. The encouraging yells turned to groans as he missed his shot.

Rip Castner grabbed the rebound and came down with his legs widespread. Then, quickly, he leaped into the air for a one-handed turn shot. It was good! For the first time in the game, Raisner was in the lead. The roar of the fans had taken a hysterical edge in those exciting closing minutes.

The face of the gym clock flashed red. Beucamp came down the floor, eager to score. Too eager. The thin-faced guard missed the pass as the play began to break. The ball bounded into the bleacher seats. The whistle blew. Raines motioned a T with his hands to Castner.

As the team came to the bench for the time-out period, the coach went down to the end of the bench where Doctor Merrill was sitting.

"I want this ball game, doc. Can Beach go in to stall it out? Is he in good enough shape for that?" He watched the physician's face anxiously.

The doctor frowned and glanced down the bench at Les. Les looked back at him with hope shining in his eyes. The doctor frowned, but nodded assent. Willing hands helped Les in getting off his sweatshirt.

As the coach gave his instructions to the guard, the players noted the confidence in his every motion. It only heightened their tension, fearful Les might not live up to his expectations.

"Okay, Les, go in and hold that ball until time runs out!"

Les heard the Raisner fans scream as he reappeared on the floor. He grinned wryly to himself as he realized his mission was far different than they expected. He found himself surrounded by two Beucamp players to prevent the pass-in from going to him. He treated the fans to a chuckle when his footwork caused the two players to collide with each other. Before they could regain their positions he had taken the ball from Ryan's pass-in and was circling close to the center stripe.

The ball bounced but inches above the floor, seemingly a part of him. He shielded it with his body as he dribbled in a tricky weaving pattern. He speeded forward as though breaking for the basket, stopped abruptly, dribbling in place, changed hands and reversed himself to go back out on the court. As he circled by the side line, he saw the Beucamp coach standing but a few feet from him. The man was gesturing wildly.

"Get him! Get him!" he screamed. His voice was drowned out by the crowd which was also screaming excitedly as each maneuver took Les in and out of the defensive court.

Number 22 advanced cautiously on Les, mindful of two-shot foul penalties. His face showed its strain. Les crooked a finger at him with his free hand, tantalizing him to come and take the ball away from him. Les whirled, sidestepped another Beucamp player who had come up from the rear, reversed again and cut around the surprised number 22.

Les came across the keyhole, dropped the ball behind him to avoid another Beucamp player and dribbled once more out of danger. Three players were now chasing him, dodging in and out, trying to hook the ball away. Now Rip Castner was standing alone under the basket. The last five seconds were ticking away.

A fourth player had now joined in the chase. Les leaped up into the air and threw an overhead two-handed pass across-court to Rip. Castner took it on the way up and climaxed the game by a neat hook shot. The gun exploded simultaneously.

Raisner fans swarmed down from their seats, jubilant and loud-voiced. Some of them crowded around the dressing room tunnel to yell at the team as they went downstairs.

"Nice going, Beach!"

"Wow, what a ball hawk!"

Although his head was throbbing, Les felt a warmth steal over him. For once no one mentioned his shooting. All they could think about after his stall was his ball handling. It was better that way, he decided with a pleased grin. Maybe he could get to be a team player!

The Tomahawks sang in the showers. Les, careful not to get his bandage wet, dug an elbow into Rip Castner's exposed ribs.

"Nice basket," he said.

The big center put his elbows down to his sides to protect his ribs, but he was grinning.

"Huh, you must have a stop watch in your head. I didn't think I'd get the ball off in time." Rip spewed water. "And by the way, mister, you didn't do so badly for yourself tonight!"

Jake Koons came out of the shower room and stopped in front of them.

"Who couldn't do well with everybody feeding him the ball?"

Les tried to keep his voice calm, but Jake Koons seemed to have a knack at getting under his skin.

"I didn't give those instructions to the team," he said.

"You sure got old man Raines wrapped around your finger."

Les clenched his fists in spite of himself. Slowly, he straightened his fingers and turned to get his towel.

Jake Koons crowded his luck by getting off a nasty laugh. Les tucked the towel around his waist and whirled around. His face was dark.

"If you'd play as much basketball as you shoot off the mouth, you might do better!"

Larry Ryan snapped his own towel in their general direction.

"Aw, break it up, you guys."

Koons shrugged and went into the locker room with his towel wadded in his hand.

"Don't ride him, Les," Rip warned.

Les looked up from zipping the beads of water from his long, muscular legs.

"Baloney. If he wants to talk tough, I'll give him something to talk about."

Rip frowned and looked after the retreating back of Koons.

"I wasn't worrying about that angle. If we're going to have a team, we're all going to have to get along together."

Les straightened and regarded his friend. He grinned crookedly.

"Okay, grandma, I'll be a good boy."

Coach Raines came into the locker room.

"Let's get dressed and get out of here, boys."

"How about letting us go to the aftergame mixer tonight, coach?" someone yelled from the locker section. The others quieted down to hear if Raines would give consent. All of them knew what a stickler he was for training rules.

"Go ahead, you boys earned it." The coach held his hands over his ears and pretended to shudder. He raised his arms to quiet them. Order was finally restored.

"Make the most of it, boys. It's the first and last one for the season." A few groans followed this announcement, but most of the boys began to dress faster.

Les heard the throbbing music from the student dance band as he came up the stairs. He paused in the tunnel entrance and looked out on the floor. Dancing couples swayed in rhythm to the music. What a different scene there had been but a half hour before!

"Looking for someone?" It was Judy.

Les decided not to tell her he didn't know how to dance. Tonight he felt he could do anything. Wordlessly he held out his arms, and surprisingly enough he found he *could* dance. Education, athletics and fun, maybe they were all fun if a fellow looked at them right!

CHAPTER NINE

IT WASN'T UNTIL TUESDAY'S PRACTICE THAT
the rift between Les and Koons almost flared into an
open fight on the floor. Rip Castner managed to pull
Les aside to cool off before the friction could cause
any actual exchange of blows, but Les didn't want to
be held back.

"Let go of me!"

Rip's voice was urgently persuasive, but he kept a
hand on Les's arm.

"Take it easy, Les. He wants you to swing on him.
You know what Raines said about any fighting on the
team. You'd be done for sure."

Les simmered down. He knew Jake had deliberately hipped him under the backboard and he could still
feel the sting of the floorburn from it. Les glanced
down the floor and saw Raines coming toward them.
The coach blew his whistle as he quickened his step.

"What is it this time?" Raines looked sternly from
one player to another.

Koons shrugged his shoulders arrogantly. He
bounced the basketball he had been holding, not
looking directly at the coach.

"Just because he missed a lay-up, he thinks someone
fouled him," Jake said.

The coach faced Les, and his eyes weren't too
friendly.

"What about it, Beach?"

Les gave Koons a disdainful look, but the heavy-set

guard kept his attention on the basketball he was bouncing. There was no use in giving an explanation, Les thought. He'd only lower himself in the estimation of the other players.

"I don't have anything to say."

"Then let's play ball," Raines snapped.

The incident seemed to clog the atmosphere. The boys were off stride. They looked at each other from time to time without exchanging words. Somehow they got through practice, but it was ragged enough to make Raines press his lips together in displeasure.

Wednesday, the practice session was spent trying to map out an offensive strategy for Friday night's game. Coach Raines placed them in different floor positions and made them walk through the plays until they had learned them. In turn, the coach showed them defensive plays which could make such an offense ineffective.

In the fast break, Raines showed them a modification of the three man down. He stressed advantages of a two man down the floor if the team got the ball off the backboard in a hurry. The first man handed off to the following player who drove in for the basket.

"Complicated ball handling hardly has a place in high school basketball," the coach remarked. "Simple, direct attack in fast-break ball should be effective. Ball handling with accurate passing is a big factor in any team's success. In this simple hand-off, for instance, the first player could set up a screen for the other. Also, he is in position for follow-up rebounding. Another choice, of course, is a fake hand-off and drive for the lay-up behind the teammate. One thing about basketball to remember, boys, is that new plays constantly arise from playing options encountered during actual games. You have to be alert to make them into points. Now, let's see what you can do."

Raines motioned with his hands to the student manager, who threw a basketball to him.

"Castner, you and Larking try it while the others watch. Koons, take the ball off the boards and throw it out to Castner." The coach pitched the ball against the glass backboard and watched Koons critically as he took the rebound.

"Take off!" Raines yelled to Castner and Larking who were poised tensely to run.

Rip caught the pass, took one bounce and threw the ball to Rog Larking while in the middle of his stride. Larking took it neatly and went up for the lay-in. The ball banged against the backboard and bounced into Castner's hands, who had followed up.

"No! No! No! Larking, I don't care whether it's practice or a game, shoot to make each shot. Don't get the habit of barging down there and slopping the ball in any old way that seems convenient to get rid of it. Ease it up there. Take your time."

Larking trotted back with Castner tagging at his heels.

"Take your time!" Larking grunted as he stopped beside Les. "First he tells me to get the lead out of my shoes, then he tells me to take my time."

Les tried to be friendly.

"He means for you to take time in releasing the ball so it won't bounce as hard as it just did."

Jake Koons snickered behind them.

"You tell 'em, coach!" There was no doubt that he meant Les.

Before Les could make a retort Raines swung his attention back to the squad.

"All right, Jake, you and Joe go down. Les, you take the rebound. Get that ball away fast!" The coach threw the ball upward in an underhand toss.

Les snared the ball almost before it had a chance to touch the backboard. He twisted in the air and drew back his arm.

"Jake!" he yelled. The ball hissed through the air at bullet speed.

The pass was clean and straight. The startled Koons quickly put up his arms, only to be bowled off balance by the terrific force of the pass. He stumbled and fell to the floor. He quickly jumped up. The red spot on his arm matched the red spots in his cheeks.

"Let's cut out the horsing around, Beach," Raines reprimanded, but he didn't turn away soon enough to hide the smile on his face.

Koons's face was mottled with his mixed fury and embarrassment. Only the coach's presence kept a fight from breaking out between the two willing participants.

"The idea," Les baited him in a hard quiet tone, "is to hang on to the ball long enough to do the team some good." Koons bit his lip and turned away.

"All right, Ralph, let's have another ball out here. The rest of you boys take positions and get a sweat up. Hit it!" The coach squatted on his heels at the foul stripe and watched the boys critically.

Fifty hard minutes went into fast-break ball. This was relieved by foul shooting, which gave way to the one-court drills. As substitutions were made new patterns were tried, and the boys relieved were sent to the showers.

Les had been kept in every combination and he was beginning to feel the effects of the strenuous practice. He batted down passes as though in a dream. The spring in his legs was snapping like a worn-out wind-up toy. Playing coach by example, Raines had told him. Les grimaced. He'd need an undertaker if this kept up! But he felt a savage pride that he was tough enough to last the route, and it gave him an inner reserve upon which to play. He still took the rebounds, scrapping with a reckless abandon that acted as a shock-absorber for the body contacts. Finally, Raines waved them to the showers. The others raced off for

the tunnel entrance. Les was content to walk more leisurely.

Jim Raines nodded to him, as did Tom Williams,
who had come onto the floor to talk with the coach.

"You're doing a good job, Les," Tom Williams said.

Les laughed wearily. Williams must have thought
Raines wasn't going to say anything, so he had taken
it upon himself to make a comment.

"Beach, you're getting better. I think you'll do,"
Raines said. The varsity coach winked at Les and
threw an arm around his assistant.

"I don't want you to spoil that lunkhead, Tom." He
said it loud enough for Les's ears, and Les knew it was
for his benefit.

Most of the team had showered and dressed by the
time Les came into the locker room. A few stragglers
were trying to nurse some hot water from the showers.
Les pulled off his playing clothes as he walked and
headed straight for the shower room. He stopped only
long enough to unlace his shoes and dump them beside the foot pan.

The stinging water, even though getting cool, felt
good to Les's tired body. It pepped him up. He began
to banter with Johnny Kerr and Bob Gray, and they
responded. A newborn respect was in their eyes, but it
was their friendliness that pleased Les the most.

It wasn't until Les was buttoning his shirt that he
became aware of the deadly silence in the locker
room. Puzzled, he looked around. Odd, he thought,
the fellows who had been dressed when he came in
were still there. Waiting, yes, that was it, they were
waiting for something. Waiting for what? Les started
to make a wisecrack until he noticed Jake Koons ap-
proaching him with a stiff-legged walk. Les flicked his
eyes to the other players. They shifted their eyes and
were obviously discomfited. Now what had Koons
been feeding them?

Les continued to button his shirt, but his new-found exuberance was gone.

"What's up?" Les meant it to be a casual question, but it sounded strained to his own ears.

"You've got a lot of brass asking what's up," Jake said.

"Don't play wise guy with me," Les answered coldly.

"I've come after my billfold, Beach!" No one could miss the flat accusation in his tone.

"Your billfold? How would I know anything about your billfold?" Les fought to keep his temper in check. He deliberately turned his back on Koons and reached into his locker for his pants.

"Yeah, how would you know?" Jake dragged it out with exaggerated emphasis. "No, you wouldn't know anything about it, would you? You're just the guy that had my lock issued to you last season. Ask Ralph Watts if that isn't so. You're the only one who knows the combination, and my billfold's been stolen!"

Les snorted disdainfully and began to pull on his pants. He choked back a gasp when he became uncomfortably aware of an oblong lump in his trouser pocket. It couldn't be! Unbelievingly, Les put his hand into his pocket. His fingers closed around the unmistakable shape of a billfold.

Koons had been watching him closely, almost with anticipation, it seemed. Jake was flashing a triumphant smile around the room for the benefit of the onlookers.

"All right, Beach, hand it over!"

Silently, Les gave him the billfold. He braced himself and faced his teammates. His eyes flashed from boy to boy. Why, those fellows actually believed he had taken the billfold. They were suspicious of him. He wet dry lips before speaking.

"I don't know how Jake's billfold got into my pocket. Most of you know I never lock my own locker. Anyone could have put it there. That must be what happened." But did they believe him? No, they didn't believe him, anyone could see that.

"Listen to him crawfish! I hate to think I'm playing with a guy who would steal from me."

"I didn't steal it," Les said. He tried to keep his voice steady. He saw he had failed to convince anyone. His face was hot with embarrassment.

Koons began to play slyly upon the emotions of the boys. Their faces, once uncertain, now flushed with anger.

"Not only does he say he didn't take it, which we can all see he has, but now he's trying to put the blame on someone else. What about that?"

Les stiffened. All it would take now, he decided was for someone to scrape a shoe. He didn't want that to happen. He'd made a promise not to get into any more fights, but this was different.

"Lay off me," Les warned. Koons cautiously backed away.

"You had the billfold. That's enough for me. We know what kind of a guy you are. You Shacktowners are all alike, a lazy, shiftless—"

That was enough for Les, promise or no promise. With a cry of rage, he leaped at Koons. He seized the heavy-set guard and sent him spinning into the lockers. The lockers swayed on their short legs and some of the boys jumped to steady them from falling on top of Jake.

"Get him! He's a thief!" Jake screeched as Les grabbed him and hauled him to his feet. He drew back his fist to smash it into Koons's terrified face, but Rip Castner grabbed him and held his arm from behind. Rip's breath was hot on his neck.

"For Pete sakes, lay off, you hothead!"

Les felt other hands pulling at him, and he wrenched free.

"Let go of me!"

He stood there, feet widespread. His breath was coming in jerky gasps. He'd take them all on, one at a time, or all at once. He didn't care. This was the way it always ended for him.

"Do you think I took Jake's billfold? Well, do you?"

Les misinterpreted their silence. Their silence was their condemnation.

Rip Castner stepped from the group.

"I don't think you took the billfold, Les."

The others said nothing. Larry Ryan looked as though he were going to change his mind, as did Johnny Kerr and Bob Gray, but they said nothing.

Les purposely ignored Jake Koons, who was regarding him with frightened eyes. Instead, he turned to his own locker and squatted down beside it. He began to jam his personal belongings into the torn brown suede bag, tossing the shoes that belonged to the school in the general direction of Ralph Watts.

Rip restrained Les as he stood up.

"What do you think you're doing?"

"Listen, Rip, you thought I had a chip on my shoulder about a lot of things. Maybe you see what I mean. I'm different from these other guys because I live in a tar-papered shack in a crummy end of town. If anything is stolen, guys like me get the blame. Well, I've had my fill. I didn't take the billfold, but these guys still think I did. Let them. I don't care what they think. They don't want me on the team, and I'm getting out of their way. But I'm not a thief!"

"Calm down. We'll get this thing straightened out," Rip said. The center faced the other players. "What do you say, gang?"

They waited too long to answer, Les thought. He slammed his locker door so hard it bounced open again. He stepped to the dressing room door and slammed it on his way out. He strode down the passageway.

Jim Raines, who must have heard the commotion, stepped from his own dressing room, but Les brushed by him without saying anything. He could hear the coach's puzzled voice calling after him, but he shut the gym door behind him without looking back. He was done. Let someone else be the workhorse!

CHAPTER TEN

LES SLUMPED BACK INTO THE EASY CHAIR and watched Judy Merrill with troubled eyes. What was she thinking? He had just told her about the billfold incident. Now he was wishing he hadn't.

"But Les, don't you see? You have to clear yourself."

"What do you mean, I have to clear myself? You sound as if you think I'm really guilty," Les retorted.

"Oh, you know what I mean. Don't get your dandruff up." Was she disgusted with him? Her voice sounded lifeless to him.

"Don't worry about it; I'm not." That wasn't true. He felt miserable about the whole affair. Just when he thought he might be getting along with the guys, see things their way a little more.

"Les, snap out of it!" Judy's voice was sharp. She had been watching him closer than he thought. Did she think he went around feeling sorry for himself? Did he? That thought startled him. He'd always thought he was pretty darned independent. And that Shacktown stuff—was that an excuse he used for his shortcomings? Because some people made a few rotten remarks about Shacktowners, had he been using it for his own alibi as to why he didn't do things in a more constructive way?

"What do you expect me to do? Go apologize to Jake Koons?

"Certainly not. If you had been keeping your ears open around school yesterday and today, you'd know there are some people who think he might have planted the billfold in an effort to get you kicked off the team. And you, big smart you, you had to blow your stack and walk right into his trap!"

"All right, cut it out, Judy. I know I pulled a boner. You don't have to rub it in. But no one knows how that billfold got into my pocket. And I didn't put it there."

"Will you stop harping about that! Have I ever said I thought you took the billfold? No, I haven't. What's the matter with you, Les? Do you think everyone is against you?"

Les fell silent. It did sound kind of silly to think that everyone would be plotting against him. Him, in particular, that is. Was a persecution complex turning into defeatism? He raised his head and looked blankly at Judy without really seeing her. He could hear Mrs. Merrill out in the kitchen making preparations for supper. He should be going. He stood up.

"I better be going." It was getting dark outside.

Judy crossed the room, bent down and pulled the cord on a floor lamp.

"Les, I was just thinking. What about Mr. Raines? Haven't you wondered as to what he might be thinking?"

"Yeah, I guess I've kind of let him down."

"You didn't go to practice yesterday, Les. The team is probably on its way over to Millford right now for the game tonight. It isn't right."

Les glanced at the clock on the mantel. The team was several miles from town by now. Heck, they might even be in Millford. It was only thirty miles over there. Why hadn't he tried to clear himself? Did he expect everyone to come running to him?

"I better be going," Les repeated. He picked up his jacket in the hallway. He held the jacket in his hands and looked at the big block R. A lump came into his throat. And he had always thought he was the tough guy! It would be great to be playing on that team.

A draft of cold air made him look up as Doctor Merrill came in. The doctor didn't see him for a moment. Judy's father closed the door hurriedly and stamped his feet while blowing vigorously on his bare fingers.

"Why, hello, Les. Didn't see you. Say, isn't the team on its way to Millford?"

Just the way the doctor said it, Les knew that the man didn't expect an answer. After all, he was the team physician. Why wasn't he on the bus, or at least, why wasn't he driving over to Millford?

"I'm not playing basketball any more," Les said.

"So I've heard. No need to rush off. I imagine Martha can scrape enough together to feed an extra mouth. You put your jacket down and I'll go check in with the missus. Judy, you can hang up your old dad's coat." The doctor shrugged off his coat and dumped it into his daughter's arms. He kissed her forehead lightly and went through the house to the kitchen. Les could hear him coming back.

"I've wangled a dinner invitation for you." The doctor pulled his briar pipe from his pocket and walked over to the tobacco humidor on an end table. He filled it unhurriedly. He motioned to Les with his pipestem to follow him into the study.

"How about stirring up a fire, Les? Dinner will be a few minutes yet."

Les took the kitchen match from the doctor and scraped it across the rough bricks on the hearth.

"Aren't you going over to Millford tonight?" He tried to keep his voice casual.

The doctor squinted through the cloud of blue smoke at him as he drew heavily on his pipe. Satisfied the tobacco was burning the way he wanted it, he sat down.

"Oh, sure. I have plenty of time. Why, want to ride over with me?"

Les didn't know how to answer that question. He felt the doctor's eyes on him.

"Want to tell me about it, Les?"

"What do you mean? Tell you about what? About the billfold, you mean?"

"Les, there's something more to it. Let's get it ironed out. It helps sometimes to get things off your chest. By the way, having any trouble from that Beucamp bump?" The doctor lifted a corner of the adhesive tape on Les's head.

"Oh, I'd forgotten I had that."

"You're lucky, but then boys recover from almost anything in a hurry."

The doctor was looking directly into his eyes.

"You know, Les, sometimes a doctor has the greatest difficulty in helping sick people get well if they have convinced themselves they can't get well. A lot of illness is imaginary, up here." Doctor Merrill tapped his forehead with his pipestem.

"Some of them don't want to be helped. Usually they get more attention from people than they would otherwise receive. They like to be the center of attention, so to speak."

Les saw through the double talk.

"Is that me, too?"

The doctor was silent for a minute. He reached over to the bookshelf and took a heavy leatherbound volume down. He placed it in his lap. There were big gilt-edged letters on it that matched the gilt-edged pages.

"A lot of people lack faith, Les. They get impatient for things to turn out well for them. They give it a try, but when miracles don't happen they call it quits. Faith is more like a test of time. You can't turn it off and on like a traffic light. Remember the first time we met? Yes, it was in church. I think you remember parts of that sermon, don't you?"

Les mumbled uncomfortably, "A few things, I guess."

The doctor turned up the indirect light and fished in his breast pocket for his reading glasses. He adjusted his glasses on his nose and opened the big Bible. His fingers flipped through the pages and began to trace lines hurriedly.

"It was taken from the Second Corinthians. Wait a minute. Here it is. Get this, Les. 'We are troubled on every side, yet not distressed; we are perplexed, but not in despair; persecuted, but not forsaken; cast down, but not destroyed. . . .'" The doctor looked up. "Does that mean anything to you?"

Les let his breath out slowly. So it had come from the Bible!

"It seems almost to have been written for me."

"For you, and everyone else who has ever become discouraged, Les. Sometimes we think the breaks are all going against us. Maybe they do for a while. Les, they always will, unless we face our problems and overcome them. Heck, Les, I'm not the preachy kind, but I'd sure be in a fix if I threw up my hands and walked off to let my patients get well the best way they could. What is that old saying about basketball— 'a good team doesn't need the breaks because it makes its own.' The same could be applied to individuals, Les."

"Yeah, only I guess I never thought about those things applying to a person as well. Doctor Merrill, I haven't told you anything that's troubling me, yet you seem to know. Am I that easy to read?"

"Les, most of us are self-centered with our problems. Nothing ever happens to anyone else like it happens to us, or so we think. They begin to magnify the longer we think about them. They can begin to warp our thinking if we're not careful. As a member of the high school basketball team, you're in the public eye more than most boys. Don't ever forget that, but then, you wouldn't, because you have already found that out. It's a privilege to participate in a sport and represent your school. Always conduct yourself in a manner to reflect credit to the school or organization that sponsors you."

"I haven't done much to make the school proud of me," Les said.

"Hey, snap out of it! What do you mean? Sure, sure, you've made a few mistakes, but that doesn't mean you have to keep on making them, does it? Why, after Friday night's game several of my patients were all fired up about a kid named Beach. It's a fact. They admired that keen competitive spirit you had and the sheer guts it took to come through in the clutch."

Les was hungry for such news. He wanted to believe it.

"Aw, you're putting me on, giving me a rah rah pep talk."

"Sure, some of that, but the other was the truth." The doctor smiled and hunched forward. He smacked his fist into his hand.

"You can't pitch that out the window, Les. Sure, there are some diehards who will continue to ride you, but you have some people pulling for you too. Stick with it, Les. Take that team to the regional tournament for old Jim Raines! That man thinks a lot of you."

Les's elation was overshadowed when he thought about his status on the team.

Judy's father stood up and stretched.

"I'm starved. How about you?"

"Yeah, I guess so. Boy, I'd like to be playing in that game over at Millford tonight."

"You can go over with me when I go," the doctor said.

Mrs. Merrill whisked birdlike around the dining room table as they sat down. She put a freshly folded napkin in front of Les. He smiled a thanks with his eyes. She patted him on the shoulder and hurried out to the kitchen.

As Doctor Merrill was in the act of taking his napkin from its ring, he seemed to think about something.

"Judy, how about being a good girl and running out to the car for me before we eat. There's a package in the back seat that I forgot to bring in." His daughter shook her head and made a remark about being absent minded, but he only winked and excused himself on the basis of old age.

Judy was trying to guess the paper package's contents as she pinched it with her fingers.

"Gee, it's getting cold outside. What is it, Dad? Something for Mother? Is it for me? Oh, Dad, did you get me one of those super blouses?"

"Put it down there. I'm hungry. Let's eat."

The doctor and his family bent their heads for the blessing. Les ducked his head down somewhat belatedly. Why didn't he remember things like that?

Doctor Merrill made a crack about learning to carve at med school, which brought a frosty glare from his wife. He grinned undisturbedly and continued to whack off generous slices of the roast.

Everyone finally had a heaping plate except Les. He squirmed uncomfortably, wondering what kind of a joke Judy's father was playing on him.

Mrs. Merrill clucked her tongue and took a quick drink of water.

"Bill, I think you're horrid. Why didn't you tell the boy?"

Her husband smiled blandly and delicately coughed behind his napkin.

"Now dear, don't get excited. I wanted Les to think some things over. Ah, here comes Judy with Les's chow."

Judy's eyes were sparkling as she put a cup of tea and two slices of toast in front of Les. He stared at her blankly. Evidently she was in on the joke, whatever it was.

"Judy, while you're up you might as well give that package to Les." Her dad pretended to busy himself with his eating, but he was watching.

Les took the package with trembling fingers. What did it contain? He broke the string and ripped the paper. His breath caught in his throat. He didn't trust himself to speak. His basketball uniform lay in his hands, the bright crimson gleaming under the lights. The big number eleven, his number in both practice and games, shone brilliantly white.

"I don't understand," he said. He looked at the doctor. His hands caressed the big numbers on his jersey.

"Jim Raines said there was no boy big enough to fill that uniform. He wants you to wear it tonight."

"Me? Wear it? You mean, I'm going to play!" Les pushed back in his chair.

"Hey, take it easy, Les. Yep, Jake Koons confessed making a plant of his billfold in your pocket while you were up on the floor. Raines kicked him off the team. Boy, I guess the air really singed from what Tom Williams told me. But there's something else I think you'll be glad to hear, so brace yourself. The boys voted to take you back on the team. They want you to play with them, Les."

Les squeezed the uniform in his hands. His eyes were moist.

"Gee, they wanted me to come back. They *wanted* me to come back. Hey! I mean, well, gee, Doctor Merrill, we don't have much time. We better get started."

"Why don't you go upstairs to my room, it's the one at the end of the hall, and change into your uniform. That way, you'll be ready when we get there. I guess I have dallied too long."

Les raced up the stairs two at a time. He found the doctor's room. He also found his brown suede bag up there. How it got there he didn't know. When he opened it, he saw the new red basketball shoes the Tomahawks wore.

"Size ten! Hot dog!"

As he turned up the shoe to lace it, a piece of paper fell out. Les picked it up and read it.

"We're sorry!"

Les let the shoe slip from his hand as he sat there trying to regain his composure. He was glad there was no one in the room with him. He brushed his hand across his eyes and smiled. Faith. It was a big word, and it meant big things.

CHAPTER ELEVEN

THE BIG CAR TURNED THE CORNER DOWN by the high school and eased onto the highway.

"You might as well relax, Les. We won't get there any sooner with you perched on the edge of the seat."

"How much time do we have?"

The doctor held his wrist down by the dash lights. "Here, look for yourself."

Les squinted at the watch and sat back reassured.

"We should make it easy," he said. He leaned back in the seat and closed his eyes. It would be nice to have a big car like this. Plenty of horsepower under the hood. In spite of himself, he must have dozed off, because Judy's father was shaking him. He yawned.

"We here already?" Something about the doctor's face told him they weren't. He sat upright in the seat.

A red flare was sputtering at the roadside. A state policeman was waving them down.

"Looks like there has been an accident, Les." The doctor eased the brake on. "Maybe we can help. Les, get my bag out of the back."

Les reared back and groped behind the seat. His fingers closed on the satchel handles. He lifted it over the seat and opened the door.

The state policeman looked relieved when he saw the two of them, especially when he noted the black bag.

"You a doctor?"

"Yes, can I be of help?"

"You bet you can! Me and my partner, he's on the other side of the wreck with a flare, was just coming in from our patrol when we heard the crash. We were afraid to touch anything, but one of the passengers was hurt pretty badly, so we flagged a motorist and sent him to a hospital. Four people and a little girl, all of them with cuts. I don't know whether they broke any bones or not."

Les saw the accident victims huddled together a few feet from their wrecked car. He followed the doctor quickly. He thought about the basketball game, but felt guiltily selfish. Those people needed help.

"Les, you take the little girl and cleanse those abrasions with antiseptic. Here, use this." The doctor unscrewed the cap from the bottle he held. Then he knelt down by the others and began to examine them with professional efficiency.

Les was thankful the little girl wasn't badly hurt. She clung to him, whimpering in a soft voice. Probably a state of shock, but he wouldn't know. Her cheek was soft against his. Trusting. That was it, trusting. Awkwardly, he patted her head and tried to smooth back her hair. He was surprised to hear her giggle.

"You're pushing my hair the wrong way. Mommy will be mad at you."

Les grinned and let her push him back on his heels. Her recovery was too quick for him to understand. He finally had to stop her from taking things out of Doctor Merrill's medical bag.

The doctor talked to the trooper for a few minutes, went back to the accident victims and talked to them, nodded his head and began to pack his bag.

"They're going to ride into Millford with us, Les. One of them has a broken arm. You'll have to hold the little girl. We'll have to hustle if we're going to get where we're going." He added that last sentence in an undertone so as not to be overheard by the others.

Before they got to Millford Les learned that the little girl's name was Sheila, she had three brothers, one puppy and three goldfish.

Sheila's mother, who sat beside Les, had closed her eyes, but Les could tell from the passing lights in town that she was in pain.

Les carried Sheila up the steps of the hospital and took her into the lobby. As he put her on her feet she pulled his head down and gave him a wet kiss.

"You're nice."

Les chuckled. No one else had seemed to think such sentimental thoughts about him. He waited for Doctor Merrill, who had gone up in the hospital elevator.

He glanced around the lobby. His nostrils tingled to the strange smells. He wanted to be a doctor. Or that was what he had thought. Yeah, all the money. He had never stopped to think about relieving people from pain, what good he might be doing for them. You had to know a lot to be a doctor, to be ready for any kind of an emergency at least expected times.

The elevator doors opened and Doctor Merrill stepped out. He stopped at the desk and left a number for the receptionist to call. The little girl tugged at his coat.

"Is my mommy all right?" The doctor smiled at her.

"As good as new in a few days. We're going to drop you off at your Uncle Harry's. Won't that be fun?" Sheila expressed delight.

The doctor turned to the receptionist.

"Is it all right? Did you get the party?" When she nodded, he asked her for directions to the high school gym from the hospital.

"Come on, Les, we better get a move on or the game will be over."

They had trouble finding a parking place, but a few fans were getting into their cars. Les saw the cars carried Raisner plates, and it gave him a shock. He stopped a man who was about ready to close his car door.

"Is the game over?"

"Over? It might as well be. Millford is leading 41 to 18. I'm going home and watch television. I never should have come in the first place. Well, I'll know better the next time." He jammed the accelerator down and raced the car motor, impatient to get away. Les backed away from the car and signaled Judy's father that he had found a parking place for him. He wished it weren't under such circumstances.

From the smokers standing in front of the gymnasium Les knew it must be the half. Doctor Merrill paid for their tickets to save time. A Millford faculty member directed them to the dressing room.

Ralph Watts opened the door to their knock. He gawked at them as they entered.

"What happened to you?" he asked Les.

"Auto accident. Not us. Someone else." Les began tossing his outer clothes in all directions. Merrill was talking to Raines.

Les faced the players. He looked at them and they looked back at him. He felt his heart pounding with excitement. He grinned and grabbed Rip's shoulder.

"Let's go get 'em, gang! Pour on the coal!"

Chatter spurted out like a gust of wind. Then they were all yelling.

"Let's go! Let's go!" chorused and re-chorused in the tiny room.

Ralph Watts looked at his wrist watch.

"Time, Mr. Raines," he called.

"Give 'em a good game," the coach barked on their heels.

Just before the referee tossed the ball into the air for the center jump, Les smacked Castner on the rump and clapped his hands. He pointed positions to the other members of the team and yelled encouragement. Something contagious swept the team, a newborn spirit, Les could feel it. The others were gripped by it. The floor general was back!

Rip batted the tip to the left. Les leaped into the air to grab it before the Miller player could get possession. He took a quick bounce and sent the ball streaking to the forward breaking under the basket. Joe Taylor hooked it into the hoop for two points.

The Miller guard threw in from the end court, but Les had snagged the ball out of the air. He faded back on his heel and dropped a one-hander from fifteen feet out.

Ryan and Les pressed the next pass-in. Larry tipped the ball over to Les, who tipped it back while both were running for the basket. It was a spectacular play, and the boys on the floor could hear the Raisner fans come back to life when the ball nestled through the hoop.

The Millford coach called time. Les could see him pointing at his number eleven as he trotted to the Tomahawk bench.

Raines grinned as the boys made a quick swipe of the towel across their faces.

"Give 'em some more of that, they don't like it. Now you're playing basketball. Les, they've been using a two man in for defensive rebounds so you shift in, and Joe, you fall back to guard with Larry. We want that ball!"

In his exuberance, Les put too much zip on a pass and lost it out of bounds.

"That's okay, Les boy! We'll get it again!" Ryan yelled.

The Raisner defense tightened. The team was alert to its scoring opportunities. Les commanded the backboards. The Tomahawks surrendered only five points to the Millers while adding sixteen to their own score to bring the torrid quarter to a halt at 46 to 34.

Les knew he was the boss on the floor. Far from resenting it, the boys seemed to love it. He set up the defense, screamed out give-aways and himself broke up Miller plays before they could get under way. He had taken a beating under the backboards, but it had given Raisner the edge needed to score. They were getting more shots, and they were hitting at a hot clip.

The Miller coach called another time-out. His face showed its tenseness. The strain was beginning to tell on him. What must have looked like easy pickings with a second-rate team had turned into a battle royal.

Raines slapped each sweating back in turn. He waved to the bench to get the other boys to talk it up.

"Eat 'em up!" the Raisner coach called after the team as it trotted out to its starting positions.

The two teams waited for the toss, all eyes trained on the ball. Once more lanky Castner got the tip and Les was there to save it. Les quickly reversed himself and dribbled speedily along the center stripe. Two players had remained behind to press him. He changed hands and increased his speed. Suddenly he stopped.

The Miller player threw up his arms awkwardly as he tried to keep from falling into Les, but the ball was already on its way, as was Les. Larking had circled out from the corner to relieve him and receive the pass.

Quick Tomahawk passes seesawed as they tried to unbalance the three men down before their team-mates could get into action. Ryan drove in and scored. He and Les stayed down the floor to harry the Millford pass-in.

Desperately, the Miller player looked for a receiver. None was in the clear, having gone too far down the floor in the haste to set up a score. Finally, as precious seconds ticked away, he threw a hard pass at Ryan's legs in hopes the ball would bounce outside and give the Millers another chance for a throw-in.

Larry stumbled as the ball struck him. The deflected ball rolled across the floor. Les hawked it on

the dead run. He fired a quick jump shot that hit the
hoop flatly but stayed in. Score, 46 to 38.

Raisner fans let out a war whoop. The tiny pep
band of five students blared into the school song. The
Tomahawks were on the march!

Millford scored, but the Tomahawks retaliated with
two quick ones from the middle of the floor. A foul
was called on the Miller forward for charging. Rip
added another point, hauling the Raisner team up to a
48 to 43 score.

Millford took another time-out to cool the Toma-
hawks. When play was resumed they went into a stall.
The clock flashed red. Raisner fans were chanting,
"Take it away! Take it away!"

Miller fans shrieked a warning to the ball handler,
but it was too late. Les had taken it away from him,
but he was almost immediately tied up. He crouched
for the toss, all muscles tensed. The overanxious Miller player went up with the ball, and in spite of the
howls of protest from the home fans, the ball was
awarded outside to Raisner.

Les took the ball from the referee and quickly
threw it down into the corner to Joe Taylor. Joe
missed his set shot but got his own rebound. He dribbled out from under the backboard and passed to
Castner. Rip had to get rid of it. Back the ball went to
Ryan, then to Les.

Les glanced up at the clock and saw the game was
lost even with a score, however, he gave the signal to
set up the rotation pattern to get the ball worked in
past the tight defense for a better scoring position.
Only seconds remained. Les calmly bounced the ball
in place.

Larking cut across the court, a Miller tagging him
closely. Les faked a hand-off and flipped the ball behind his back to Castner. Rip took the pass high on his
way up into the air. His pivot conversion was the last

shot of the game. Score, Millford 48, Raisner 45.

Instead of bowing their heads in defeat, the Toma-hawks raced off the floor yelling like Comanche Indians. They knew something now they hadn't known before. Tonight they had found out they were a team!

CHAPTER TWELVE

LES STARED INTO THE MICROSCOPE AND adjusted the mirror underneath the platform for better light. He shifted the prepared slide with his thumb and forefinger until he had located the best view of the specimen. It was a stained slide of the flatworm, showing all three cell layers. Keeping both eyes open, he peered through the monocular eyepiece with his left eye. He raised his right eye occasionally to the drawing he was making. Behind him, he heard Mr. Harbison reminding a student to keep both eyes open while looking through a microscope. It was a hard trick to learn and required concentration.

The biology teacher stopped beside him, watching him at work. Then, apparently satisfied, he moved on to the next lab table.

Across the table from Les, Rip Castner snorted in disgust as he pushed his microscope away from him. For a moment, he watched his teammate in his concentration.

"Hey, doc, come out of it!"

Les looked up, but ducked his head to go back to his observation. That was too much for Rip.

"What good's this stuff ever gonna do us?" Castner griped.

"About as much good as basketball will do us when we're fifty years old," was Les's rejoinder without looking up. His pencil was moving slowly.

Rip leaned on his elbows after taking a cautious look over his shoulder.

"Tell me, Les, do you really go for this stuff?"

Les turned his head sideways to look at Rip.

"Yeah, I guess I do. I'd like to be a doctor some day."

"Like a certain party's old man, for instance?" Rip dug good-naturedly.

"Something like that, maybe." Les erased a line on his drawing and blew the eraser crumbs across the table.

"Why don't you be a coach, like me? That's what I want to be. You'd be a natural," Rip said.

"I don't know. Funny thing, Rip, I even have a different slant on being a doctor lately. I used to think of all the big money. After that accident the night of the Millford game, I found out that doctoring was more than making money."

"What do you mean? The hard work and all that stuff?"

"Sure, there's hard work, all the studies and long hours, but I'm thinking about another side of it. People. You help people. I never thought about that before. Maybe I'm turning soft."

"Soft? What do you mean soft? The way you climbed my frame under the backboard a few times, I wouldn't call you exactly soft!" Rip hastily turned his attention to his microscope as the biology teacher looked up and moved toward them. He was detained by a student who wanted help. With a warning glance at the two boys, he bent down to focus the microscope for the girl.

The class bell brought Harbison erect in a hurry. It must have dawned upon him that he hadn't given tomorrow's assignment. He started to say something, but too many students had streamed from the room in escape. He shrugged resignedly, but upon seeing Rip's happy expression he couldn't restrain a grin of his own. He motioned good-naturedly for the boys to get out, which they did with Rip an easy first.

Les met Judy at her locker.

"Hi," he greeted her. He was beginning to be more at ease with Judy.

"That's original." She closed her locker and they began to move slowly down the hall.

"Say, I don't have a biology assignment tonight. I can get my other lessons in study hall easy."

"What's all this leading up to?"

"There's a pip of an adventure picture down at the State. I thought that, well, you know, maybe we could see it together."

"A movie? Les, I'm surprised at you."

"You mean because I'm an easy spender with all my money?"

"No, you sap! I mean about basketball. I thought you were in training." Judy stopped walking to look up at him.

"What's that got to do with it? I've got it all figured out. We can get there when the show opens and still be home by 9:30." Les was losing some of his good spirits.

"It isn't right, Les, and you know it. I'd love to go with you, but I don't think I should. You know you boys aren't supposed to date during the week. 9:30 really doesn't have much to do with it. Why those boys are playing their hearts out to have a good team. They're counting on you. Wouldn't it be fine for you to be strolling around town when you should be at home?"

"Cripes, Judy, I can't understand you. What harm can there be in a little relaxation? I won't be doing anything wrong—not like times last year. I always play hard. You know that." Les put his hands on his hips and frowned.

"When you're out for basketball, Les, that should be

the uppermost thought in your mind. Basketball. Nothing else should interfere."

Les was on edge. He spoke before he thought.

"Including you?"

"Including me," Judy said. There was a defiant air about her that he couldn't understand.

"Okay!"

"Okay?"

"Yes, okay! If you don't have time for me, why didn't you tip me off sooner?"

"Oh, Les, don't be muleheaded. Try to understand. I'd think you would after other things that have happened to you."

"And what do you mean by that crack?"

"Listen. Try to understand. I want you to be at your best at all times. One date during the season would only lead to more. After a while it would begin to mean later hours. It would affect your playing basketball. Les, try to understand." Judy's voice was now soft, almost pleading.

"Try to understand, you tell me!" Les exploded.

"Quiet down, other people are looking at you," Judy said in a fierce undertone.

Although Les had very limited experience in going with girls, he recognized the proper time to get off his high horse and make concessions.

"But after basketball season? Okay?"

Judy's eyes became mischievous.

"That's a long way off," she teased.

"Good grief, Judy, don't you care at all?"

"Don't be silly," Judy called back over her shoulder as she ran for her classroom.

"Don't be silly," Rip's voice simpered behind Les.

Les whirled around.

"You're not funny!"

"Aw, take it easy, Les. Where's your sense of humor? You have one of the nicest babes in school crazy about you—if you don't fly off the handle." Rip's sincerity as well as a trace of envy couldn't be mistaken.

"You know what? I can't even get a date with her. She says it's no go during basketball season. What do you think of that!" Les fell in step with his teammate.

"I think you're lucky, that's what."

Les snorted.

"Lucky?"

"Yes, I said lucky. What about those gals that date the guys on a team on the q.t. and then get the boys in hot water with the coach? Or the townspeople start a whispering campaign about you if you're not in training? Heck, I thought you were wised up by now."

"Yeah, I see what you mean. I hadn't thought about that. All I could think about was that I've really never had a date with Judy."

"Huh, what do you mean you've never had a date with Judy? Who do I see strolling out of the church together these Sundays? Whose big feet are always parked under the Merrills' dining room table?"

Les tried to keep the pleased embarrassment off his face, but he couldn't.

"Remember, Les, all it would take to wreck our team is for that first guy to step out of line. So far no one has, to my knowledge. I wouldn't want you to be the first one, if you get what I mean." Rip turned into the library with Les.

Les flashed a quick grin at the earnest center.

"You know, Rip, I think you might make a pretty good coach at that—that or a preacher!"

"Better make it a coach," Rip said dryly. He appeared satisfied, however, that Les had seen his point.

"I'm going to check out a hunting and fishing magazine to take home for Dad," Les said.

"Lucky dog. I have to look up some history references. See you at practice." Rip drew his hand across his neck as though he were going to the gallows. Les shook his head and walked over to the magazine rack in the corner.

He flicked open a magazine that had an interesting cover. He found himself thinking over the things Rip had been saying. He backed into an empty chair and sat down.

He hoped Rip had been right about Judy liking him. How could he see her without breaking training? Maybe he had better let well enough alone and keep things the way they were. Sometimes Judy would repeat parts of Reverend Maynard's sermons, the parts, he guessed, to which she thought he had missed the point, the parts that should do him the most good. Then there were always those Sunday dinners. Well, he liked the doctor, and he suspected the feeling was mutual. Mrs. Merrill seemed to look upon him favorably. Funny, people like the Merrills taking a liking to him, a guy like him, especially after some of the stories they must have heard about him by now.

Without looking further in the magazine he took it to Miss Garr, the school librarian, to be checked out overnight.

The woman drew her eyebrows together.

"Tell me, Les, do you ever study?"

Miss Garr was also the senior class sponsor. She knew he had one of the best averages in the school.

"Feverishly," Les said. He almost laughed aloud when she made a face at him.

"Pooh!" she said in a very unteacherish manner. She took the card from the back cover of the magazine, marked it and put it into the file on her desk.

"It's for my dad," Les admitted, as he indicated the sports magazine.

"How's the basketball coming along?" The librarian's eyes gleamed with an interest that surprised Les.

"We're getting better," Les said. It had been an offhand remark, but after he had said it he recognized the truth of the statement. The boys *were* sharpening up.

"That's what I thought," Miss Garr nodded her head. "I've been to both games."

Les couldn't mask his surprise. Somehow, he'd never thought of Miss Garr as a basketball fan.

"You have?"

Miss Garr studied his face a minute before she spoke. She seemed to choose her words carefully.

"Ever since my sister's boy started playing basketball on the hoop against the garage up until he made All-American several years ago, I've followed the game. You know, Les, you remind me of him. Charles Raney, only I think the sports writers used to call him Coz."

Everyone interested in basketball had heard the name of Coz Raney!

"Coz Raney! The All-American! Aw, Miss Garr," Les said in embarrassed pleasure.

"I watched Charles develop, Les. You two have the same general characteristics, speed, skill and good rebounding. You know, Les, the more I think about it the more I think you have it in you, but that's up to you to decide."

"Say, what happened to Coz? He made All-American in his junior year in college. I don't remember reading anything about him after that. What happened?"

Miss Garr indicated the library assistant's vacant chair at the side of her desk.

"Sit down, Les."

Much against his will, because of the snickers from students, Les slid down into the chair. The librarian turned to him.

"Coz got the big-head, Les. He thought he was the whole team after he made All-American. He drifted in his studies. Frankly, he flunked out."

"What? Oh, a college wouldn't flunk an All-American, Miss Garr." Les laughed uneasily. He was thinking about the significance of her remarks. Not the flunking out, but the other similarities.

"That college did," Miss Garr said. She rapped a ruler on her desk to restore order. That was the only side of Miss Garr most students ever saw—Miss Garr, the disciplinarian.

Les sat still. Was she preaching to him? Why did everybody feel they had to preach to him? Good gravy, it got tiresome. Flunk an All-American? Aw, she was spoofing him! As he stood up, the librarian also rose to her feet. She was considerably shorter than he. Les felt resentful as he looked at her.

"Why tell me these things?"

"You have brains if you want to use them, Les. You have ability to play basketball. The day of the dumb athlete is over. Keep cracking those grades. Play as a team member. You have untapped capacity. When you make the decision for yourself, nothing will be able to stop you."

Les couldn't help but feel the magnetism in those clear blue eyes. He had never noticed it before. He'd always thought she was a rather drab little character. She was sincere. She liked him, and in her way she was trying to help him.

Later, Les told his dad about the conversation he'd had with Miss Garr. His father listened silently. He seemed deep in thought. Finally, after staring into space, he looked up at Les.

"You know, son, you must have some good stuff in you. Must come from your mother's side of the family. A lot of people take an interest in trying to help you."

"Yeah, especially lately—"

His father seemed to anticipate what was in his mind.

"Go ahead, finish what you were about to say."

"Well, what I mean, well, good gravy, Dad, since I got going in basketball, everyone seems to want to hop on the bandwagon! Yeah, but where were they last year?" Les tried to choke back the words, but they had been locked inside too long. They spilled out in a torrent he couldn't check.

His father came out of his chair with a bound. His eyes were blazing.

"Now, you listen to me, young man! Last year you didn't deserve anything but a kick where it would have done you the most good." Then the implication of his own words came to him. He breathed heavily. Father and son stared at each other, separated but an arm's length. Then his father waved his hand in the air and turned around with a shrug of his broad shoulders. He sat down, almost wearily, and rubbed his hand across his face. Les could hear the scratch of his whiskers.

"I'm sorry, son. No, I take that back. Maybe we both had it coming to us. I guess I just got sore hearing you talk like that. I can see your side of it. Heck, ain't you old Sam Beach's son?" His dad looked at him quickly. Les wondered if his dad were afraid he might resent the comparison. Well, maybe he had for a minute, he wasn't sure.

"It's okay, forget about it, will you?"

"No, I'm not forgetting, Les. What you don't know is that a lot of people have been working quietly in the background for you—some of them before you fired the first shot this season. I wasn't going to tell you."

Les looked at his father strangely.

"What do you mean?"

"Why do you think the town bum got a job? Haven't you ever wondered about that? Miss Wheeler talked me into taking a job with her brother so you could have more free time for doings down at the school. Your buddy Rip Castner's the one that called the showdown on that billfold trouble. Went right to the coach, he did. And there are others—"

"What do you mean by others?" Les was half-doubtful, half-curious.

"Don't forget your friend Doc Merrill! I can tell by what you say and by certain things you do that he has made an impression on you. He likes you, Les. Then there's Elmer Robbins down at the store. He's pulling for you. Don't forget, he gave you a job when nearly everybody in town was sour on you. There aren't many people who would do that."

Sam lapsed into another silence. He got up and put another slab of wood into the stove. He watched the flames licking at the wood before he looked up at Les.

"Tell me, son, did a particular sermon in church make any sense to you?"

Les was caught by surprise. He hadn't expected a remark like that—not from his father! Then it came to him. Les felt the excitement building up within him. He spoke the words aloud, hesitantly at first, then as his father nodded understandingly, he repeated the entire quotation.

" 'We are troubled on every side, yet not distressed; we are perplexed, but not in despair; persecuted, but not forsaken; cast down, but not destroyed. . . .' "

"That's the one," his father said.

"What about it? Dad, I have to know!"

"Think back. Remember when Bertha Wheeler got you to promise to go to church that Sunday? She posted Reverend Maynard to preach that particular sermon because you had told her you would be there."

Les felt paralyzed by weakness. All of this coming at him—all at one time! What if he hadn't gone to church that Sunday? Had there been a change in him? What had he thought about during that sermon? When and where had he said, "It seems to have been written for me!"

CHAPTER THIRTEEN

LES WAS UNABLE TO SLEEP MUCH THAT
night. Incidents of the past ran incoherently through
his mind. People's names and faces flashed again in
his imagination. There were voices too, some of them
from the past. These voices were related to a particular night when the fans had ridden him almost out
of the game. Fred Owens' bull-like voice seemed to
rise above the others.

He felt a vague uneasiness when he thought of
Fred. This was a part of his life he was trying to forget. When he thought of Fred, old guilts returned to
bother him. Another feeling, equally discomforting, an
undefinable dislike for the man grew from a bitterness
of remembered experiences where the older man had
made him the scapegoat because he was the younger.
Or was it because he was weak?

He twisted under his covers and tried to think over
what his father had said tonight. There were people
trying to help him. Why? Did they have some kind of
a missionary complex? Who would suspect prim, old-
maidish Miss Wheeler would be thinking enough
about him to try to help him? *He* never would have,
he admitted to himself. In the background there were
Doctor Merrill and Judy. Another name came into his
mind. At another time he wouldn't have allowed it to
be on the credit side. Now he knew it had always belonged there. Coach Jim Raines! What was it he had
said the night of the Beucamp game? "I can remem-

ber a time when a skinny black-haired kid would have
killed giants for me." That kid was bigger. What
would he do for him now?

And there were others his dad hadn't mentioned.
Even the fans seemed to be accepting him. More im-
portantly, to his own mind, the boys on the team had
accepted him. To think they had actually voted to
have him come back on the team!

Almost guiltily he recalled another person who had
lent his aid in a quiet, dignified way. Reverend Maynard. Why was it he had almost forgotten him? Was
that the way it worked? A fellow only thought about
church and religion when things bothered him and he
needed help? Were they last resorts?

By sitting up in bed he could look out upon the thin
layer of snow that lay like a flimsy, moth-eaten blanket on the weedy yard. If he leaned forward slightly
he could see the dim yellow reflection of the light that
burned so continually in Billy Horton's bedroom. He
moodily thought about Billy, but when he lay back
again to stare up into the blackness of his own room
other thoughts crowded the boy from his mind.

Then there was Dad. He was always there. Maybe
he took him too much for granted. It had been hard
on his father to recount his own mistakes. Les had to
give him credit. He hadn't spared himself. Les felt a
comfortable closeness and pride in his father he hadn't
felt before. So Dad had broken down to get a job so
he could play basketball! Les tried not to grin when
he thought what a problem that must have been for
his dad to consider.

And about himself. A fellow couldn't reform all at
once, it seemed. A guy had to do a little backsliding
before true values asserted themselves enough to
mean anything. No, that couldn't be right. A fellow
only complicated his own life by not seeing things
sooner than he did.

This was his last basketball season at Raisner High

School. The time to produce was now. There would be no second chance. The truth of one of Rip's statements suddenly crystalized. If he were to get the most from basketball he had to give a part of himself to it. He had to be a team player. By himself he would get nowhere. Why had he been so blind to such a simple little fact as that before?

The next morning Les toyed with his spoon in the oatmeal as a thought began to assemble into recognizable shape. He looked at his father, who was shaving over the kitchen sink.

"Dad, I want to do something for Jim Raines. I spent a lot of time thinking about him last night. I don't know what I can do, exactly. He's been pretty good to me in lots of ways."

His father wiped the straightedge carefully on a piece of toilet paper and turned away from the mirror. He stirred his hand in the shallow water of the basin beside him to clean off the blade before he spoke.

"That so? Seems you were singing a different tune than that last year."

"Yeah, I know I was. A guy can change his mind, can't he?"

"You're asking or telling me?" Sam chuckled. He swished the blade in the water again and pulled the skin of his face taut as he tilted his head.

"Okay, have your laugh," Les said.

"Shucks, son, it's easy to see what you should do. I'm surprised you haven't thought about it yourself." His dad turned around, still holding the straightedge at right angles to his face.

"You mean, win that sectional tournament?"

"What else? You know how that man has lived for the day he'd win just one sectional."

"Then we'll take him all the way!" Les threw his spoon into the empty bowl as he jumped to his feet.

"Don't get all het up, Les. I'm sure a little old sectional would suit old Jim to a T-waddy." His father faced the mirror again.

"Yeah, everybody is supposed to be tough this year. Maybe we'll be lucky." Les thought about his team-mates.

"Don't sell that team of yours short. They've got spirit. Most I can remember seeing the last few years. Town people are talking about it, too. That's a nice bunch of boys, Les. They're learning, coming along real fast, I'd say."

"We're going to win that sectional. You just wait and see." Les gulped down a glass of milk.

"Tournament time is quite a ways off yet."

"Well, you know what I mean," Les said. He took his jacket from the back of the chair and slipped it on. He could hear his dad laughing as he shut the door behind him.

Les waited impatiently until the third hour biology class. He wanted to talk to Rip. As usual, however, Rip was the last student to wander into the room. Unflinchingly, the big center walked past Mr. Harbison's frosty glare and took his lab seat.

"One of these days Harbison will blow a fuse," Les whispered.

Rip unexcitedly flipped his biology book open.

"Let him," he grunted.

"Well, forget him for a minute. What do you say we talk some basketball?"

"Now you're talking," Rip said. He straightened up with interest.

"Rip, what do you think our chances are in copping the sectional?"

"I don't know, Les. I've wondered about it, but gee, it's so far away."

"Let's start thinking about it. We're going to have to eat, sleep and drink sectional tournament," Les said.

"Why all the sudden interest in the sectional? Of

course, we want to win it if we can, but heck, Les, we have a lot of games to play yet. We'd be lucky to win most of them."

"What's the matter with you, Rip? I never expected to hear that kind of talk from you. Don't talk ifs, talk like we're going to do it. To be a winner, Rip, you first have to believe it inside."

Rip regarded him curiously.

"Boy, you're the old competitor, Les. But you know we guys have a lot to learn. I want to win, but I don't want to smoke pipe dreams."

"From now on, Rip old buddy, let me dish out the fight talk. We can go places, so get on the merry-go-round." Les felt the excitement building up, but Mr. Harbison's tap on his desk with a ruler brought him back to earth.

The locker room buzzed after practice. Rip must have talked to some of them, Les thought. He waited until all were dressed before he motioned them into a circle around him.

"All right, can you guys do it? Can you win the sectional?"

Some of them laughed nervously.

"What about Appleton, last year's regional winner?" Roger Larking said. Others nodded their heads.

"What about Raisner?" Les returned coolly. The way he said it had an effect on them. They began to whoop it up. Their eyes began to shine hopefully. They were a green team, and they needed someone to fire them up, Les could see.

"That's telling 'em, Les!" Larry Ryan pounded him on the back.

Les held up his hands to quiet them.

"Hold it down, you guys. Raines and Williams are on the other side of the wall in the coach's dressing room."

The boys quieted immediately, each feeling like a

conspirator. One or two were frowning in a worried manner.

"I don't know how you guys will take this, coming from a guy like me, but I'm going to say it anyway." Les paused and searched the faces around him.

"C'mon, out with it," Paul Sears muttered impatiently.

"Okay, it's short and sweet. I play to win. I think you do too. Most of you have at least one more season to play after this one. I have only this one. We have the makings of a good ball club if we all work together. Something like Raines said once, 'It takes desire to win'—to keep giving it all you have until the gun ends the game.'"

The boys nodded their heads.

"I've been a headache to Raines, as most of you know. Maybe it's a little late, but I want to be on the team that wins a sectional tournament for a pretty good guy. I used to think I could do it by myself. I know now I was sadly mistaken. It's going to take all of us. How about it?"

"Count me in!" Rip yelled. Others joined in the chorus.

Les quieted them again.

"We all know the story about Raines. He's coached in every little one-horse town in the state, but he's never won a sectional. Let's bag a tournament for him before he retires in June. Sort of a blaze of glory for him, so to speak."

"He's an all-right guy," Joe Taylor said.

"But what about that Appleton outfit, Les? They're going like a house afire. Some sports writers are already picking them as having an outside chance of winning the state," Johnny Kerr said. His worried tone sobered some of his teammates. They looked down at the floor.

Les smacked his fist into the palm of his hand and jumped on a bench. His voice was fierce.

"We can take them!"

Grins broke out around him as spirits were once again uplifted. Les knew some of them weren't really convinced down deep inside, but it made them feel better to hear him talk that way. They might not realize yet that he really meant it.

"We have to play together. I had to learn the hard way, and I'm not very proud to tell it. We need team play, the kind that develops the savvy that automatically tells us what a teammate is going to do, where he'll break, before he does it. I'll pledge to do my part." Les's voice shook with the intensity of his feelings.

"Let's go get 'em!" The Tomahawk war whoops rent the air as the boys gave vent to their emotions.

Bob Gray started a war dance around the bench Les was standing on. The others, some of them feeling foolish, laughed and yelled as they shuffled into line.

"Scalp 'em!" Ted Haskell brandished an imaginary tomahawk in the air.

As the week's practice slipped away, Les noticed a pensive gleam in the coach's eyes that had not been there before. Raines summed up his feelings to the boys one night before the game.

"You boys have more drive, more speed. You have some kind of a fierce determination you didn't have. You still make mistakes, plenty of them; but boys, you're improving fast. You know, we just might win that sectional this year."

The boys looked at each other and guffawed, but there was a speculative glint in their eyes that hadn't been there before.

CHAPTER FOURTEEN

WHEN FRIDAY EVENING GOT OFF TO A GOOD
start with the reserves eking out a slender 49 to 46
win for their first victory in three starts, the varsity
felt it was a good omen for the game to come. When
the varsity got on the floor the fans, who had already
been whipped up by the fast-moving evenly-matched
reserve game, gave thunderous greetings to their
teams.

The Wininger regulars were wearing purple and
white, even down to their shoelaces. Even the basketballs which they used in the preliminary warm-up
were painted in their school colors.

While the crimson-clad Tomahawks were warming
up, Raines motioned to Les to come over to the bench.

"All set?"

"We're primed for bear."

"That's the spirit. I thought you boys were ready by
the way you were talking it up before you came up on
the floor. They're keyed up, but if they begin to get
ragged from the excitement, slow the ball up, Les.
Take your time if you have to. Work that ball in. Keep
that Wininger team guessing. You're the floor captain,
Les. I'm counting on you." The coach shook hands
with him and let him go back on the floor.

The first quarter moved briskly, and the Tomahawk
fans shouted their approval as their team built up a
thumping 20 to 5 lead. From time to time, when the
play had slowed down, Les had heard his name both

praised and derided by indecisive fans. They still thought he shot too much.

At the beginning of the second quarter Raines pulled Les and put Paul Sears in his place.

"Paul needs experience," Raines said. The coach tossed his sweatshirt to him, and Les put it on and sat down. He watched Sears lose possession of a rebound he should have had.

The Wininger five, playing a smothering five man rebound defense, began to command the backboard both offensively and defensively. Les had been getting the rebounds in spite of them, but Paul Sears didn't have enough experience to take good position when he had the chance. But Paul tried, and Les yelled encouragement.

The Wininger score began to mount in spurts. Finally Raines signaled a T with his hands. Ralph Watts met the team with towels.

"Listen, you guys, get the rebounds for a change, and that team is wide open for a fast break. Castner, get the lead out of your shoes. And Rog, you and Joe could help out instead of standing flat-footed while you gawk at the ball. Get those rebounds!"

Rip flashed a quick look at Les on the bench, but Les only grinned and shrugged in return. This was small consolation to Castner.

The half ended on a 29 to 22 score, Raisner still leading. The Tomahawks had been held to a thin nine points while the Wininger Bears had galloped within hailing distance with a good seventeen-point quarter.

In the locker room, Raines gave instructions in a tight, clipped voice. Players sheepishly hung their heads as he singled them out with his criticism. They felt worse knowing he would just as liberally praise them if there had been anything to praise them about. Les watched them to see their reactions. For once, he mused, he wasn't on the receiving end.

"Good offense starts at backboard control," Raines

reminded them. He nodded at the door and they broke from their cramped positions, eager to get away from the stinging tongue of Jim Raines. Les fell in step with the coach on the ramp.

"Les, I want those boys to learn to play without you, just in case they have to sometime. Wait it out for a little while, but if they get into any more trouble you're going back in."

So that explained that. What did Raines mean by the "just in case they have to sometime"? He shook his head as he took his place on the bench beside Bob Gray. Of late he had been sitting between Gray and Raines. The coach would make low-voiced comments to him from time to time during the game play, expecting him to remember the right things to do if those situations arose again.

The third quarter was more evenly matched. The Tomahawks were doing better at rebounding, which was all that preserved a slender 46 to 40 margin as the teams came into the homestretch. Raines had let Sears start the fourth quarter, but he turned to Les on the bench.

"Okay, Les, I want you to get out there and take control of that team and the ball game. You can do it. Watch that big forward for fouls."

Les could hear the spectators buzzing excitedly as he replaced Paul Sears. They gave Paul a nice hand.

Les gave Joe Taylor the sign for him to drop back to his guard position, and Les moved up into the forward's spot. Larking cut loose with a shot from his favorite corner, but the ball hit the back of the iron. Les grabbed the ball and came out with it, bending low and twisting to get away from the surrounding Wininger players. Quickly he flipped a half-court pass to the speedy Ryan, who had seen him get the ball and had moved out accordingly. Larry's lay-up was good.

Time after time the same play was executed, sometimes involving two or three quick passes, but always ending in a basket for Raisner. Tardily the Wininger five shifted into a three-out, two-man-in zone on defense, but the damage had already been done.

The game ended with the Tomahawks on top, 65 to 46. Les's dad told him later that plenty of Raisner fans remarked how his rebounding seemed to be the difference, and not the twelve points he had scored. Besides, they said, Les had only played two quarters, hadn't committed a personal foul in spite of his rebounding and had only allowed the opposing player three points.

The team members chattered in the showers, mindful only of the victory. Les slipped carefully into his trousers, letting the cloth slide gently over his skinned legs. He felt a momentary resentment about the floorburns and twelve points. Maybe tonight, if Raines had left him in the game, he could have broken the home floor single game thirty-point scoring record. Just as suddenly he was ashamed of his thoughts. Ideas like that had given him the boot from last year's squad! It was difficult, he acknowledged to himself, to listen to the others talk as though they had won the game by their personal point contributions. They forgot who set them up to fire those shots.

Les saw Raines watching him with quiet amusement, and he flushed. The coach must have read his mind, he thought uncomfortably. He reached for the doorknob as Raines spoke to him.

"Good night, Les. And by the way, that was one sweet game, fellow."

That was what Les wanted to hear, but it made him mutter an embarrassed reply. He couldn't remember later what he said. It didn't matter if Jim Raines knew. That was all that counted. He almost collided with his father when he opened the door.

"Ready to go home, son?" His dad gave his shoulder a proud squeeze. His dad knew, and Les's spirits were uplifted.

"You bet I'm ready to go home." It had been a good night.

As Les stepped into the cold air, a serious, freckle-faced junior high boy thrust an autograph book in his face. Les drew back in surprise.

"Wouldja sign it, please, huh?"

It was the first request of that nature Les had ever had. He almost pushed the boy aside, but he thought about another kid who used to hang around the gym after ball games to see the varsity players. His fingers trembled as he signed his name on the smudged page. As he returned the book to the boy, he didn't know why he did it, but he reached out and ruffled the boy's hair. Maybe it was a physical relief for his feelings. He was rewarded by a wide-mouthed grin of big teeth.

"Boy, you sure can play basketball," the freckle-face breathed in heavy hero worship. Les looked at his dad and was surprised to see tears of pride in old Sam's eyes.

"Come on, you sentimental sap, let's get home!" But Les linked his arm in his father's as they walked down the school drive.

Elmer Robbins greeted him by calling him "champ" when he reported to work the next morning. Customers stopped to talk to him or once in a while one of the men would wink at him from the check-out line at the cashier's counter. It made him feel good, like riding on clouds. He worked as though in a dream. He whistled as he walked home that night.

His father was just leaving the house when he turned into the yard.

"Where you going?" Les asked.

"Now, Les, you know I go down to the firehouse on Saturday nights to play euchre with the boys."

"Yeah, I guess I forgot. Thought maybe we could talk over last night's game," Les said.

"Aw, forget the game, it's over. I left some hot dogs

heating on the stove for you. The beans are probably still warm." Les was puzzled by his father's slighting reference to the game. It became clear when he finally found the newspaper in the coal bucket where his dad had tried to jam it out of sight.

He had begun the account of the game with eager eyes, but they frosted as he went through the article. Finally he flung the paper on the floor and glared angrily through the kitchen window. His jaw muscles tightened. He was confused.

Only passing mention had been made of him. What comment there had been was tinged with a tongue-in-cheek reference to his last season's playing. Why did the sports writer have an ax to grind with him? Couldn't that blind bat see he was now a team player?

Les ignored the water bubbling around the wieners and let it boil over. He scooped the paper from the floor and reread the sports column carefully. Rosy references were made to Larry Ryan, a "comer," a scoring machine that had sparked the Tomahawk attack with twenty points against Wininger. Twenty badly needed points.

Oh, yes, there was a smug comment about Les Beach, a player who seemed to be on his back more than he was on his feet. Les rubbed a skinned knee gingerly as he read that and abruptly threw the paper toward the coal bucket. He jerked the pan of boiling water from the stove and put it on the drainboard. He wasn't hungry.

Again he replayed each minute he had been in the game. He searched for errors he might have made. But Jim Raines had said, "That was one sweet game." Had he misunderstood the coach? Had Raines been referring to the team as a whole? That would be more like the coach. What about the junior high autograph hound? Had the kid been looking for just any basketball player to sign his autograph book? Had he been kidding himself in his new role?

Les thought about the time he had pledged to be a team player. Were the guys laughing up their sleeves at him and using him for the means to build better reputations for themselves? Was he the fall guy?

What a big sap he had been. He should have known better. You had to look out for yourself. Nobody was going out of his way to help you. You had to do it on your own. He'd run those guys into the ground. They wouldn't make a fool out of him. Big stars, yeah, big stars!

He threw himself in a chair and hooked his leg over the chair arm. His day was coming. But he was disturbed more than he wanted to admit. Words Doctor Merrill had said to him kept coming back to break into darker thoughts. Things didn't happen all at once just because a guy gave them a try. You had to keep at it. How long? How long did a guy have to give out before he got anything back? Was he ever to get anything back from his efforts? By golly, they'd sit up and take notice if he broke the gymnasium scoring record! Somebody besides Larry Ryan could grind out the points!

CHAPTER FIFTEEN

THE FLAME OF THE TOMAHAWKS SEEMED
to die away after the Wininger game. The team was
ragged. In spite of that, the Raisner five managed to
stay on the heels of their opponents. The losses were
heartbreakers with low scores. One loss had been by
one of those frantic, but lucky, three-quarters of the
floor last second heaves. Another loss had stabbed
them in a sudden death overtime. The most recent loss,
against the powerful Appleton five had been by the
slim margin of three points. The total spread of points
given up by the Tomahawks had only been a scant
seven points in the three games.

Les had not been particularly encouraged by the
close Appleton game. He believed it to be one of the
Tigers' worst games. Then there was the small feeling
inside that he could have done more rebounding instead of loafing around the edge of the keyhole to
have additional shots at the basket.

It had all begun with that write-up after the Wininger game. He knew a coolness had somehow sprung
up between the team and himself. Nothing definite,
but that vague feeling was there. They sensed a
change in his attitude, but no one had said anything
openly about it.

Les felt he had tried to salvage the Appleton game,
but he had come too late with too little. It rankled
him that Sage, the Tiger guard, had outscored him.
Sage had slipped around him twice. Sure, that could

happen to anyone, but Les knew he would have to play better ball than he had during that game if the Tomahawks were to win a sectional tournament.

Rip's remark after the Appleton game had cut him deeper than he wanted to be hurt. He could still see Rip's puzzled glance as he said, "Les, I was wide open for an easy shot. Why didn't you pass off?" Rip had laughed awkwardly, trying to cover up, but he hadn't fooled Les.

During the week's practice Les could feel Jim Raines's eyes boring into his back. When the varsity coach drew him aside during Thursday's light scrimmage, Les knew the coach had him tagged.

"Les, I want to talk to you. Let's go to my office." Without waiting, the coach started walking toward the end of the gym. Wordlessly, Les followed. He was conscious of the low-voiced comments from the team, but he couldn't distinguish what was said. He felt a strange tension as he closed the office door behind him. It didn't help any when Tom Williams rose to leave. Raines must have said something to him, because the assistant coach gave Les a bare nod as he left the room. Then they were alone, just he and Jim Raines.

Raines sat with pressed lips, drumming his blunt fingers on the desk top. The chair creaked as he sat upright.

"Les, you're short-changing me. You're short-changing yourself."

Les felt uncomfortable, but he tried not to show any sign that he suspected what the coach meant.

"What do you mean?" His voice sounded insincere in his own ears.

Raines's keen eyes narrowed.

"You know what I mean! Let the other guy do some of the work—you want to do the shooting. That's it, isn't it? Just like old times, eh, Les?"

"That isn't fair! You know I've done better for you this season."

"You've lost three ball games for me this season," Raines snapped.

"I have? I thought you always told me there were five men on the floor. What about them?" Les had almost convinced himself he was in the right. But it made no impression on the old coach.

"Les, I've tried to be fair to you. Against my better judgment, I took you back on the team. You showed flashes of cooperation—" The coach shook his head.

"I suppose you're giving me the boot again, is that it?" Les said hotly.

"Listen, hardhead, if I kick you off this time, I don't even want you in the gym as a spectator." The man's voice had taken a shrill pitch, and Les knew Raines was trying to control himself.

"All right, so I'm a glory hound. Is it so wrong to want to make good? I take the elbows, the shoves—all the rough stuff, but the other guys take the credit. They get the points."

"One of the boys told me you were really sold on team play. What kind of baloney did you dish out that time?"

Les stopped his next retort short. The sounds of his breathing filled the tiny room.

"The trouble is, I really meant it. I know you won't believe me, but I really did. I wanted to do something for you. I don't know, I'm all mixed up."

"You usually are," Raines said dryly.

"I guess it all started with Larry Ryan getting the credit for the win over Wininger. Carney wrote me up as some kind of a bumpkin, and I didn't like it." Les felt better now that the admission was out in the open. He raised his eyes again.

"Les, do you know what Larry said to me after you left that night?"

Les shook his head.

" 'Mr. Raines,' he said, 'boy, how I wish I could hawk a ball like Beach does it. Gosh, I couldn't have scored if it hadn't been for him.' "

Les stared at him unbelievingly.

"Ryan said that?"

Raines only nodded his head. Les felt pinched inside, a small feeling that kept getting smaller.

"Les, it seems all I do with you is to preach. This afternoon I want you to make a decision. You decide for yourself if it's worth it. You play as a team player, or you turn in your suit. We'll lose games without you, games maybe we should win. But we're losing games with you, so it makes little difference. Think it over a minute before you decide. Whichever way it is, this is the last chance."

Les caught his breath in his throat. Always the ultimatum. There was no halfway. He thought about the boys on the team. There had been some pretty good times with those guys. Their overtures of friendship, only to be baffled by his attitude. Once they had voted to have him come back to the team. They had shown a certain kind of faith that had meant a lot to him. Had he let them down, made them more bewildered than ever? Why did he have so many ups and downs? Why did he slip back into his old ways? He reached his decision.

"I want to play."

"Les, you need basketball and these boys. These boys need you. Give some of yourself and get something bigger and better in return. They haven't quite decided what is wrong. They think they know. Show them how wrong they are."

"I'll try," Les said.

"Go get your shower before you catch cold, and be on time at the gym tomorrow night." The old man's voice told him nothing as to how he really felt. It had that reserved note in it, the kind that said, You have to show me.

Rip Castner was the only one in the locker room when Les entered. Les avoided looking at him, not knowing what to say. He knew Rip was watching him closely.

"Stick around, Rip, I'll walk uptown with you. Only take a minute." He took his shower quickly and dressed. Rip hadn't said a word, just sat there staring at him, like he was trying to figure him out. When Les held open the door, he passed through it without turning around.

"Think we can take that Bayfield outfit?" Les tried to make his voice hearty. He couldn't think of anything else to say.

"Yeah, I guess so," Rip said. His voice was lifeless.

"Rip, wait a minute. I want to talk to you."

Rip stopped and waited expectantly. His face showed strain.

"Rip, I slipped out of line again. I know it, you know it and the guys all know it. I turned headline hunter because I didn't get a big write-up. I know I was wrong."

"So?"

"Rip, you're the only friend I feel I have. I don't want to lose that friendship. Try to forgive me, or whatever it takes. It takes time, Rip. A guy can't just change all at once. It's hard, Rip, honest, it's hard!"

The tall center watched him closely, a slight relief showing in his eyes. Then Castner broke into an embarrassed grin and started walking.

"C'mon, hothead, we'll be late for supper."

Les started talking all at once, little things, eager to fill that dismal gap he had felt a moment ago. But Rip understood. Rip could tell when a guy meant it. Rip was a pretty good guy. He didn't say anything. He just grinned, but it made Les feel good.

They reached the town square and stood on the corner waiting for the traffic light to change.

"Let's stop in at the Hangout, see who's there," Rip said.

In a way Les hoped none of the team members were there, then again, he hoped they were. As it turned out, Ryan, Taylor, Kerr and Larking were hanging over a rear booth teasing some of the girls. They looked up when Castner and Les clapped them on their shoulders.

"If it isn't the All-American," Larking laughed.

"Lay off, Rog. Les's okay," Castner said. He dug an elbow into the forward's ribs.

Les saw them exchange the barest flicks of their eyes.

"Larry, Raines told me what you said after the Wininger game," Les blurted. Ryan jerked up his head. The little guard was cautious.

"Yeah?"

"I want to thank you. I only hope I can do as much for you again."

The fellows shot another quick glance around. Then they grinned.

"Have a glass of water on me," Ryan said. He slapped Les on the back and Les knew that once more he had been allowed to enter the group as one of them. This time, Les promised himself, he was in for keeps.

When the girls finally cleared out the boys crowded into the booth and began to talk about basketball. Les lost count of the glasses of water they drank. He also lost track of the time.

The early evening crowd began to drift in and the boys were reminded it was long past suppertime. They glanced at the clock over the counter and began to shove each other out of the benches.

"Let's get out of here. My mother will skin me alive," Johnny Kerr said. The others laughed, but they didn't lose any time themselves.

Les talked with Rip a few minutes at the street corner, but finally Rip told him he had to get home. As Les walked leisurely down Chestnut Street he tried to recall what had been so pleasant about the afternoon. Nobody had really said anything important, but it seemed to him it had been one of the best times he had ever had. He began to whistle as he walked.

There was a lot more to basketball than just playing the game.

CHAPTER SIXTEEN

LES STOOD OUT AT THE CENTER STRIPE with Rip Castner as they warmed up for the Bayfield game. Both turned to watch the Bayfield Bears taking their lay-ups.

Rip shook his head.

"Boy, are those guys big! I'll bet there isn't a one of them under six-one."

"Yeah, they're big, all right," Les admitted. He was paying attention to the careless flop of their elbows under the backboard.

"How big would you say that center is?" Rip said. A worried frown marred the usually good-natured face.

"Must be ten or twelve feet tall," Les said. He laughed and ducked the swing Castner took at him.

"Boy, I sure hope Raines moves you up to the boards," Rip said.

"Don't worry, he probably will," Les returned. He held his hands out and received the ball from Joe Taylor. He bounced it, took a deep dip with his knees and sent the ball arching through the air. It banged against the iron and shot almost straight up into the air. Les met the high bounce on his follow-up by tipping the ball into the basket.

"Nothing worries that guy," Rip said to Taylor.

"Don't kid yourself! Les just keeps it down inside," Joe said. The forward shifted his gum in his jaw as he began to break for the backboard.

A referee came into their court and Les met him. A

Bayfield player was with the man. The boys introduced each other and shook hands. The referee gave them instructions.

Les turned away and went to the bench. Raines was smacking his fist into the palm of his hand as emphasis for what he had been saying.

"Defense—defense—defense! This Bayfield outfit is big and rough. If you begin to pull away from them, watch out for roughhouse. They're known for it. Play clean ball.

"Another thing, you boys have tried the little hero routine and it cost us three ball games. If any of you can get set, fire for the boards. Make sure that backboard is covered, though. Don't worry who makes the most points. Scorekeepers are hired for that job. The first boy who forgets what I have just said gets benched.

"Keep a hand in their faces all the time. Keep yelling at them. Throw a press on them, full court, if they get within two or three points when you're in the lead. Do you hear that, Les?"

"Got it," Les said. And in that moment, he knew he had "got it." Raines was telling him something between the lines. The coach might as well have handed him a blueprint reading, "I'm wise to you, get back into line." Les flashed a look at the surrounding faces. He was surprised the others seemed to be getting the same message. Well, those things were ironed out now, but Raines wouldn't know. The boys grinned at each other over the coach's back as he squatted in their midst.

The Tomahawks banged three quick field goals into the payoff column before Bayfield made a point from a foul called on Larking. Rog protested the decision, but the referee handed the ball to the Bayfield forward and motioned for Larking to get up to the foul lane. When Larking caught an elbow in the face as he went up for the rebound, he was really angry. He

turned to the referee, but the referee was watching
the ball and didn't pay attention to him.

Then the game began to get rough!

As the Tomahawks came in to the bench for the first
called time, Les saw Williams was having his hands
full keeping Jim Raines under control. The old coach's
face was red.

"Why does Sarse allow his team to play that kind of
ball? Someone's going to get hurt out there. I'm
protesting to the referees."

"Calm down, Jim," Williams said. He was pulling
Raines back to the Tomahawk bench.

Les glanced down the row of seats to see how Sarse
might be taking all this. The Bayfield coach was grinning and slapping his players on the back. When some
coaches were caught without material, Les knew, they
would let almost anything get by. The Bayfield rough-
ing was a deliberate attempt to throw the Raisner
team off their game. And they were succeeding. The
almost inexperienced Tomahawks were getting jittery
and losing their tempers.

Les wasn't complaining. Being an old hand at rough
stuff, he knew he had given back more than he received, but he also knew Jim Raines wouldn't approve
of it even if they had been behind ten points.

"All right, boys, slow the ball down. We'll cut down
on this barnyard stuff right now. If they foul us, we'll
take the points instead of getting clobbered under the
basket and getting nothing." The coach had thrust his
chin out. He pushed Tom Williams' arm away.

Play was resumed. The Raisner team moved the
ball slowly, forcing the height of the Bears to move
out from under the backboard. The deliberate time-
consuming tactics weren't to Bayfield's liking. The
center, a husky two hundred and twenty pounds,
hipped little Larry Ryan and took the ball away.

To the screaming, protesting Raisner fans' surprise,
no foul was called, and the center went the full length

of the floor to score his lay-up. Ryan was reeling groggily as Les slipped an arm under him.

"I'll get that big stiff for you, Larry," Les promised.

Bob Gray replaced Ryan and Les waved him into position. Gray was somewhat taken aback to see the angry gesture he made, Les knew, but it wasn't because Gray had come into the game, as he probably thought.

A foul was called on Les when he hipped the big center into the side lines. But the center only grinned viciously and wiped his hand across his mouth. His expression said, "I'll get you!"

Les lost track of the score, so intent was he in nailing the big center. He caught three more personal fouls, but only two of them had been because of the Bayfield player.

The center stopped at Les's guard position before he stepped into the jump circle.

"Tough guy, eh?"

Les faced him with cold contempt.

"When I leave this game, you're coming with me."

It happened on the next play.

A loud "Ohh!" gasped from the Raisner crowd as Les was hipped into the first row seats. Frightened spectators scrambled to get out of the way as Les came hurtling into their midst.

Les flung up his arms to avoid falling into people and twisted so as to land in the most thinly occupied area. Almost as soon as he crashed into the hard edge of the seat boards, he was clambering to his feet. His eyes were blazing with wrath. He couldn't hear Jim Raines shouting for him not to get into a fight, as others told him later the coach had. All he was conscious of was the "Get 'em, Beach!" he heard from the men clustered around him. He didn't need their encouragement. He had already made up his mind as to his course of action.

He could see the grinning features of the Bayfield

center, and that was all he needed. The center ducked the first punch as Les came in with both fists slamming like air hammers. He caught the center on the jaw with his left and had to step forward hurriedly to get his right into the follow-up.

The Bayfield center's face went blank as he sprawled awkwardly on the floor. As he got to his feet, a thin trickle of blood coming from his lip, Les hit him again. This time he stayed down. Les hovered over him.

"Get up! Get up!"

The roar of the crowd swelled about the frantic whistle blasts of the referees. The Bayfield crowd was yelling protests, but the Raisner fans were screaming at Les to take them all on. Tonight, after the crude fouling against little Ryan, their sympathies were with the hair-trigger guard who was now swinging at any Bayfield uniform that came within range.

Another Bayfield player skidded on the floor, but grabbed at Les's legs as he went down. Les wrenched his foot away from him, but caught a fist in his eye as he was pulling away.

Fans surged out on the floor and the pitiful handful of local police, who had anticipated nothing but a free basketball game, were almost snowed under by the avalanche.

Les lost track of the minutes, but he knew he was the target for almost every Bayfield fist swung. He met the onslaught willingly, but he knew he had taken on more than he could handle. His right eye was almost completely closed. Blood coursed freely down his face. He could feel the cuts inside his mouth also bleeding.

Several attempts were made to calm the crowd over the P.A. before they finally cleared the floor. Les swayed on his feet, ready to unleash another fist toward a tormentor, but Rip Castner grabbed his arm from behind.

"Let go of me!" Les commanded hotly. Rip wrestled grimly with him, not losing his hold.

"Take it easy, Les."

"I'll smack that monkey into next week's game," Les snapped.

The big center was still lying on the floor, but he was struggling to get to his feet. He didn't make it and collapsed to his knees.

Joe Taylor grabbed his other threshing arm and hung on grimly.

"You already have," Joe said.

The referees bent over the Bayfield player and helped him to his feet. Just seeing him on his feet made Les want to hit him again, but he was too weak to make the attempt.

Sarse, the Bayfield coach, pushed the referees rudely aside to get a better look at his player. He walked stiff-leggedly toward Les. The Raisner fans roared angrily.

"Just what did you think you were doing?"

Rip and Joe dropped Les's arms and tensed at his side.

"Ask that big lug what he thought he was doing to our other guard a while ago."

Raines, puffing heavily and followed by Tom Williams, ran between Sarse and the Tomahawks.

"My boy's leaving the game, Sarse. I don't condone unsportsmanlike conduct, but I think your boy got everything he had coming to him. We don't play dirty basketball here. I'm glad this is the last year of our contract." Then the old man turned to the referees.

"If you had been doing your job this rough stuff wouldn't have happened."

Les stepped to the old man's side and balled his fists.

The referees stepped between them.

"We've had enough of that here for tonight. Both you coaches get back to your benches. And as for you,

Raines, we call them as we see them. Now, let's get on with the game."

As Les draped his sweatshirt over his shoulder and walked to the bench, he heard a mixed chorus of cheers and boos. He made no sign that he heard them. He sat down beside Raines, who turned to him with a strained look on his face.

"My golly, Les, I thought you had that worked out of your system. Sure, I backed you out there, but you know how I feel about these things. You're not going to do us any good warming a bench. Self-control, Les, you'll need it long after your basketball playing days are over. Hang on to that temper before it really gets you in bad."

Les ran his tongue lightly over the inside of his mouth, feeling the rawness of the cuts. He shook his head.

"I lost my head. I'm sorry. That is, I'm sorry about all this mess, but I'm not one bit sorry I poked that big stiff."

Raines swung around to make another reprimand, but something made him grin unexpectedly. He squeezed Les's shoulder.

"My gosh, but you're a scrapper!"

Les was wondering if the old man had suddenly re-membered that he had stepped to his side when it looked like more fireworks were about to go off.

"Get your shower, Les. Better soak that eye for a while. Boy, that's going to be one beaut of a shiner." The coach returned his attention to the game.

Les paused in the tunnel entrance and a grin stole over his face. The playing on the floor now looked like tiddlywinks compared to the earlier part of the game. He glanced up at the scoreboard and saw the Toma-hawks were leading by ten points. Bayfield was tamed. They'd never catch them now. Satisfied, he went down to take his shower.

At half-time Les listened while Raines gave instructions to the team. Larry Ryan winked at him from across the room and it made Les feel better about not getting to play the rest of the game. Larry was in the lineup again.

Raines said a few things about sportsmanship, and how he didn't want any repeats on the performance of a few minutes before. He said he and Sarse and the referees had gotten together and ironed things out. He made an excuse for his fellow coach by explaining the pressure on him back in Bayfield, but he didn't magnify it. He said they had to be examples of the best of sportsmanlike conduct at all times.

Les wished them luck as the team filed out of the room. Doctor Merrill lingered a moment to look at his eye.

"You'll be all right. Les, I know you feel in your mind you did the right thing, but force alone never solves anything. Under the circumstances, I'm not blaming you too much, but don't let it happen again. The fans become pretty much emotionally involved. Someone could have been hurt. That's not why we have basketball in the schools. Think it over, Les." The doctor gave him a friendly wink and closed the door behind him.

Les stared at the door and sat down to put on his shoes. It felt funny to be kicked out of a ball game. Not funny exactly—odd, maybe that was the word for it. Why was he always so belligerent? Was there something wrong with him? He couldn't stand being pushed around.

He thought about the old Shacktown gang that had raided the gang clubhouses across town. He had looked forward to those battles. He had been socked with rocks, walnuts, tin cans or anything else a boy could throw. He'd thrown his share of them, he admitted to himself.

Those days seemed so recent—yet he was now a senior in high school. It was time to grow up. In just a few months he would be working at some job around town and maybe later he could go to college to be a doctor. Yeah, fat chance he had to go to college! That temper of his would get him into serious trouble if he didn't whip it soon. Surely he was smart enough to figure a better way to solve his problems without feeling he had to tear someone's head from his shoulders. He looked at his skinned knuckles and shook his head.

He didn't know what drew his gaze to the faded sign hanging over the doorway. CLEAN SPORTS. The school Hi-Y had placed it there years before, he supposed. Funny, he couldn't remember ever having read it before, yet he knew he must have. He spent more time reading the fight signs plastered around the locker room walls. Signs like that had more pep to them.

Good grief! If he kept up this moping around, he'd never get to see the rest of the game. He roused himself and went out to the playing floor. He took a seat next to Ted Haskell on the end of the bench.

The scoreboard read, Visitors 47, Home 63. Only three minutes remained. Raisner, with a safe lead tucked under its belt, had gone into a stall, content to let Bayfield chance two-shot personal fouls trying to take the ball away from them.

The Bears did finally break the stall, but they were unable to score. Castner took the rebound from an almost docile substitute for the big Bayfield center. Rip passed to the corner where Ryan waited for it.

Larry flipped the ball to Taylor, who drove all the way and brought his point total to fourteen for the evening.

The Tomahawks threw a full court press on the pass-in from out of bounds. The Bear forward was tied up for a jump ball.

The gun exploded as the ball left the referee's hands.

Ted Haskell stood up.

"Too bad you didn't get to play the whole game, Les," he said.

Les wondered what he would have said if he had been in Ted's place. Ted didn't see much action in the games.

"They managed to win without me. Hurry up and get your shower. Rip and I will walk uptown with you, probably some of the other guys, too," Les said. He gave Ted a push toward the tunnel. The lanky substitute stumbled, but a happy grin was on his face. Heck, Les thought, he's as much a part of the team as any of us!

CHAPTER SEVENTEEN

LES HAD WAITED AS LONG AS HE DARED BE-
fore getting a haircut. He disliked the tight cloth
around his neck, the incessant snick, snick, snick of
the scissors and the sleep-inducing heat.

Charlie Stevens had cut his hair since he'd had to
climb up and sit on a board rested on the arms of the
chair. Charlie grinned and nodded his head toward
the chairs lining the wall. He stropped the straightedge razor. Les sat down to wait, hoping it wouldn't
be too long. One good thing about Charlie's shop was
the wide assortment of magazines he kept for his customers. Les picked up a picture magazine and began
to leaf through the pages with unhurried carelessness.

The customer in the chair, who had been stretched
out horizontally, a hot towel steaming over his face,
was raised to a sitting position. It was Fred Owens.
Fred looked under Charlie's moving arm and saw Les.

"How's the local flash?" He gurgled on the last word
as Charlie toweled his face.

Les looked up from his magazine cautiously. More
than once he had recognized Fred's bull-like bellow at
the home games.

"So-so, I guess," he said. He tried to use a tone that
would discourage conversation.

Fred raised an eyebrow as he rolled his portly body
in the chair so he could take out his money.

"Haven't seen yuh down at the smoke shop this

year. You used to be one of my best customers, didn't
you, Les?"

Les bit his lip without answering. He and Charlie
exchanged a quick look as they saw the fat roll of
greenbacks Fred pulled from his pocket. Fred, pre-
tending not to notice, peeled a bill from the roll and
jammed the rest of the money in his pocket with a
careless shove.

"You seem to be doing okay without my business,"
Les said.

"Yeah. Yeah, guess I am. Lots of little peanuts make
lots of leaves. Drop around. That is, if you aren't forgetting your old friends." Fred shrugged into his overcoat.

Les got silently into the barber's chair. Charlie
frowned as he flipped the cloth out over his customer.

"Why don't you quit riding Les?" Charlie said. He
was looking directly into the fat man's face.

Fred lost some of his good humor. He turned from
them while putting a hand out for the doorknob.

"Charlie, you stick to your barbering. Les and me is
old buddies from the same side of the tracks. Ain't
that right, Les?" He seemed to get some kind of pleasure when Les avoided looking at him.

Owens changed the conversation abruptly.

"What are our chances in the sectional this year,
Les?"

"You've seen us play," Les said as he hunched his
shoulders.

"That's no answer. Well, drop in one of these days
to chew the fat, big shot." Owens shut the door behind him. From the outside he took the time to laugh
at Les through the big plate-glass window.

"Why doesn't that guy leave me alone?" Les turned
his head for the electric clippers.

"I don't know, Les, but he's up to no good. He re-
sents you, Les. He sees you getting accepted and he
can't quite make the jump from Shacktown to Cross-

town. He thought he had a hold on you from some of those old Shacktown scrapes. Fred is the kind that likes to have others knuckle under to him. Like those parasites that hang around that pool hall of his, guys looking for a quick buck from an easy spender. You're too independent for him."

"Yeah, I suppose you're right. Well, I've forgotten him already."

Les might have forgotten Fred Owens, but the pool hall-smoke shop proprietor hadn't forgotten him, as Les found out Wednesday night after practice. Les was inwardly distressed to see Fred sitting in the big hardtop convertible at the curb in front of his house. Owens was smoking a cigar and reading while he waited. Fred lowered the paper as he turned the page. Les felt trapped without knowing why. He approached the car.

Fred opened the car door and let it swing wide. His cigar butt hit soggily in the gutter. Fred patted the upholstered seat beside him.

"Get in," Owens said. He kept patting the seat.

Les felt his face harden, knowing Fred saw it too.

"It's about time we got together, Les. So you don't like me, so okay, but I have something that might interest you. There's some paper money in it for you."

"Lay off, Fred. I'm not interested," Les said. He stepped back from the car. Owens lunged halfway across the seat. His voice had lost all pretense of friendliness.

"Get in, wise guy! I'm not talking pennies to you, this is real dough, the kind you lay awake dreaming about!"

"What do I have to do? Not that I'll do it, understand?" Les stood back from the car.

"I'm not going to shout it all over the neighborhood. Get in and we'll cruise around the block. You want to drive this bus?" Fred scooted over to make room for him.

Les wasn't going to get into the car. He half turned away. Was that Rip Castner down at the next corner? Fearful that it was, he jumped into the car and slammed the door behind him. He didn't want Rip or any of the guys to see him talking to Fred Owens!

"Step on the gas! Let's get out of here!" Les half-crouched to peer through the windshield. It wasn't Rip down the street. Too late now.

Observing his behavior, Fred chuckled. Les was too disgusted with himself to make a retort. He slumped back in the seat.

"Head for the country," Les said.

"Okay, so we'll go out into the country a little ways so some of your new friends won't see you with me," Fred said. He had been watching Les with narrowed eyes.

"Cut the smart talk and step on the gas," Les said. He let himself slump in the seat. He turned the radio switch, but Fred snapped it off. Plainly, there were more important things on his mind.

"I've got some information straight from the capital city, Les." Fred lowered his voice confidentially, but he kept his eyes on the road.

"Such as?"

"Word's gotten around. Certain people know about you. Big people. The right people. That interests you, huh?" Fred must have seen him sit up straight.

"What are you peddling, Fred? I'm just a small-town ballplayer. Don't try to kid me." Even in the semidarkness, Les couldn't quite mask his curiosity.

"Thought that would get a rise out of you." Fred shot him a quick glance and slowed the big car's speed.

"Some of the big city sports writers have been scouting around the bush leagues looking for local color stuff, or whatever those newspaper guys call it. You were good enough when they first saw you for them to look you over again."

"So what? Maybe I get a couple of inches of type."

"You don't see it? Listen, Les, high school basketball is bringing in big money. You ought to know that. Basketball pays the whole athletic bill in most of the high schools in the state. Football, track and baseball are just fillers until basketball season rolls around again."

"You don't make it very clear as to what you're driving at. Turn the car around, I want to get home."

"Okay, so we can the build-up. Every hick is a sentimental sap and bets on his own ball club. He thinks his loyalty is questionable if he doesn't pick the local yokels to win a sectional, so he puts a chunk of dough on them. Smart guys move in and clean up."

"And you're one of the smart guys?"

"Right! Wise up, Les. For example, supposing you got a little something for winning. There wouldn't be anything wrong with playing hard for the school to win—and still cash in for a little gravy. You wouldn't be throwing games. I'm asking you to do something you would do anyway. Isn't that easy dough?"

Les was conscious of a tightness in his throat.

"What's all this have to do with the malarky you were spreading about the city sports writers?"

"Listen, Les, they're looking for big things from that little ball club you're on. You're the difference whether they go anywhere. I didn't know myself how good you were supposed to be until I got the word." A tone almost respectful crept into Fred's voice. He tapped Les on the shoulder with his free hand.

"You go along with me on this, Les, just like old times, and I can make myself a nice piece of change and you can get enough for that med school expense. Or don't you want to be a doc anymore?" Fred was unemotional about it. Like it was in the bag.

Les was disturbed by the insecurity of his own emotions.

"It isn't honest."

Fred was patient.

"Don't play boy scout with me, Les. You're talking to old Fred. We know each other. Sure, I'm trying to tie onto something big for myself, but I'm looking out for you, Les. Don't forget, when you were a snotty little kid you used to hang onto my coattails. I'm trying to help you, kid. I'm tipping you to the big money. Money that will buy big things—things a guy like you wants in life. And you play it to win. Easy, ain't it?"

Fred took out a pack of cigarettes and offered one to Les, but Les shook his head. The fat man didn't insist. He reached down and punched in the car lighter and waited until it popped out to light his own cigarette. He took a deep drag, letting the smoke suck down into his lungs. Les licked his lips and wondered whether a cigarette would taste good after the long time he had been without one.

"Aren't you fellows taking a big chance on Raisner going very far?"

Fred exhaled with a snort.

"Les, wake up, kid." Fred jabbed him with an elbow. "Don't you realize you're probably one of the greatest high school basketball players in the state?"

"Basketball takes five men, sometimes ten or twelve, Fred."

"Horsefeathers! That's rah rah kid stuff, Les. I'm surprised a bright guy like you falls for that baloney. Wise up, I tell you. Cash in."

Ashamedly Les realized his mind had been ringing like a cash register. Oh, not that he would actually do it, he tried to rationalize for his own peace of mind, but he estimated the different uses to which he could put the money. Again he tried to be stubborn, almost fearful at his own thoughts.

"It isn't right."

Fred became silent. He steered the car along the highway. Les heard the tires purring over the concrete. Fred studied him for a minute. Then he broke the silence as he turned off on Chestnut Street.

"Let's refresh your memory. You play your heart out —for what? You get banged up—for what? Next year they'll be yelling someone else's name. You'll be a past issue. Maybe you'll be packing groceries for Elmer Robbins then, listening to the other guys getting the pat on the back. Do you want to keep reminding yourself the rest of your life what a sucker you were when the big dough was there for the asking? Not many guys get the chance I'm giving you, Les."

As a timed climax, the car stopped in front of Les's house.

Les started to get out of the car. Suddenly he felt unclean. He wanted fresh air. He wanted to get away from Fred Owens before he accepted the proposition. He was detained by Fred.

"Wait a second, Les. If you're worrying about the moral angle, chew this over for a while. The farther that team goes, the more you'll make. What do they want in these basketball towns? A winner! You bet they want a winner, not in Raisner as much as some, but they don't pay big salaries to coaches just to furnish something the school band can play for. Don't forget that."

"Why proposition me at all, Fred? You know I play to win."

"Call it a little bonus to make sure you won't forget to win," Fred said. He was purring like a cat. Fred knew he had him tottering.

Les jerked open the car door. A few snowflakes drifted into his face.

"Let me have some time, Fred."

Owens rolled down the window and leaned his head through the opening. Every line of his face became crystal clear.

"Sure, Les, sure. Let me know tomorrow. Drop in at

the smoke shop. I'll be there all day. Play it smart and keep this confab to yourself. It's your protection, so to speak."

"I don't need a diagram," Les snapped.

Fred didn't take offense. He rolled up the car window and shifted gears. The big car pulled away from the curb and took the pitted holes in the street with easy shock-absorber action.

Les clenched his fists and stared after the convertible until its taillights winked at the railroad crossing. Still he stood there. He could get a car like that if he was smart. Yeah, and move out of this tar-paper shack he and his dad called a home. Even if Fred had painted a rosy picture, which he probably had, there would be enough for things he really needed. Things like a new suit of clothes. Maybe he could get an orchid for Judy to wear at the Senior Prom next June. She'd like an orchid.

And all he had to do was to play a little basketball. He marveled at the simplicity of it. Oh, he'd have to collect a few more floorburns, hog a few more buckets and keep the team jumping—but he did all those things anyway. If he handed Jim Raines a sectional champ, the old man would be in seventh heaven. Everybody got helped. Everybody, that is, except the suckers who bet the wrong way.

CHAPTER EIGHTEEN

LES TOOK A DEEP BREATH AND TRIED TO steady himself before he went into the house. What was the matter with him, anyway? He clenched his teeth and tried to feel cocky about the unsuspected attention he had been getting from the sports writers. But the hurt kept gnawing inside. Here was the chance to kick over some of this Shacktown stuff that always clung to him everywhere he went. Here was a chance to dress like other people. Even go to college. Be a doctor. Yeah, make big money.

His mind flashed back to the highway accident the night of the Millford game. Doctor Merrill hadn't been thinking about fees that night. The doctor had taken care of the situation and gone about his business. There had been no mention of money.

Les thought about his elementary school days. He'd had to go to one of the schools across town. He was always different from the others. Not only in the way he had to dress, but there was something about him that made the other kids leave him out of things. He was never invited to any of the school parties. The girls stuck up their noses as though he really had a disagreeable odor.

Again Les felt the discomfort he had felt as a boy waiting to be chosen on sides for scrub baseball or group activities in the classroom. Oh, in sports he was usually one of the first three or four chosen, but in the classroom he was one of the last. Like being the extra piece of a jigsaw puzzle that didn't fit in anywhere. He had tried to act like it didn't matter, but the hurt built up inside.

When some of the boys began to repeat remarks they had heard at home about old Sam, the town bum, he began to get into fights on the school grounds. If there weren't too many of them ganging up on him he usually won those fights, but they were empty victories. No one changed toward him. He wasn't accepted.

He spent hours mastering the spelling lists and arithmetic tables so he could beat them in the classroom. That had been the beginning of his better grades in school. His consistently high grades in class had relieved some of the pressure from the teachers, but that was all. They tolerated him. Nothing more.

There were a few bright lights, maybe. Take for instance old Mr. Murray, the shop teacher. Les had liked the kindly old man who usually had a good word for him. He'd send Les into the print shop and let him work on the school paper, setting the type, because he knew Les didn't like to work in the wood shop. Mr. Murray would just laugh and say he didn't have any wood to spare for a young wood butcher to work on, but the way he said it, with that twinkle in his eyes, you knew he wasn't sore at you. Les had been sorry when Mr. Murray had retired.

Heck, it seemed the only fellows that took an interest in him were the old men about ready to retire. Take old Jim Raines, for instance. Raines had tucked him under his wing to develop him into a basketball player back in the junior high days. Now the coach was ready to retire. This was his last season. He'd have to stop thinking about Jim Raines. The sense of guilt was too strong when Les thought of those high ideals held by the coach.

Les wondered even now why Raines had seemed so

unreasonable—to expect so much from him—to blame him when things went wrong. He had called Les the troublemaker of the squad in those earlier high school days. That was it. Always, he was the troublemaker. He was always the guy out of step.

"We are troubled on every side, yet not distressed; we are perplexed, but not in despair; persecuted, but not forsaken; cast down, but not destroyed. . . ."

Why had he heard those words? They dinned thunderously in his ears. Why was he so soft underneath? Why be a sucker? Why fight the odds when things he had always wanted seemed to be within reaching distance?

Les half-stifled a sob as he turned from the front door. Through the window he could see his dad puttering around in the kitchen. There was a newborn pride in his father since he had been working regularly and bringing home a weekly pay check. Heck, Dad was even daydreaming about saving his money so he could buy a little piece of land from Leonard McKee up on Cane Creek. It would be a big blow to his dad if he ever found out about this Fred Owens deal. But he didn't have to find out, Les told himself fiercely.

Finally, jamming his hands deeply into his pockets, Les began to walk. He didn't know why he was walking, nor where he was going. He only felt a driving intensity that had to be exercised.

He walked the three-block length of Shacktown once, twice. His teeth chattered as he saw the little houses shivering so nakedly beneath the snow-covered roofs. The thin wisps of smoke from their chimneys made him think of the slab wood he and his dad burned at home because it was cheaper but not as warm and lasting as a good coal fire.

When he had been younger, he and his dad went down to the fire station during long winter evenings when even the wood supply had been limited. Those

had been pleasant, drowsy hours until his dad had
gently awakened him to take him home—and into the
cold darkness of the night.

Les looked up to get his bearings. He was almost in
front of the Hiltons', which meant he had looped back
and was almost home. Just seeing that grim little
house made him think again about Billy. He really
should see the kid sometime. It was really the neigh-
borly thing to do.

What did Ernie Hilton have to show for his rightful
living? A tar-paper shack that wasn't even his own, a
bare back yard where a few chickens scratched, a bro-
ken-down car that didn't run anymore. Yeah, he could
see the jalopy rusting away beneath a light covering
of snow. Les shifted his gaze from the car back to the
house. Yeah, and a little boy who had been sick for a
long time.

Hesitantly, he knocked at the Hiltons' front door.
Why? He didn't know. Just to see how Billy was coming along. Should have stopped by before. But why
now? He'd only stay a minute.

Ernie Hilton smiled wanly when he recognized Les.
His gaunt cheeks were dark from several days' growth
of beard. Nervously the man ran his hand over his
face as he closed the door behind Les to shut out as
much cold air as possible.

"Nice of you to come over, Les. How's Sam?"

"Oh, Dad's okay. Been working over at Wheeler's
sawmill, you know," Les mumbled. Now he was wishing he hadn't stopped. He had enough problems of his
own without being reminded of other people's troubles. The whole house had a depressing effect on him.
Les's eyes swept the room. Just like his place. Same
kind of stove squatting in the center of the room, surrounded by chairs over whose backs clothes were
draped to dry so as to be worn clean again the next
day. Same old warped floorboards ridging the worn
linoleum that covered them. The smell of kerosene

mingled with the smell of cabbage. It sickened him.

A cracked mirror hung crookedly over the water bucket and basin. Les was startled to see the mirror reflect the picture that hung across the room. The Lord's Last Supper. One of those prints you could get from one of the magazines for a quarter.

This was Shacktown, he told himself bitterly. This was the life he himself knew so well. This was the life from which he was going to make his escape.

Ernie Hilton had been watching the basketball player uncomfortably, as though he could read his thoughts, Les felt. Mrs. Hilton came through a curtained doorway and just stood there. She looked tired. Discouraged. She blew a straggling wisp of hair back from her face.

"Want to see Billy?" she asked.

Les, without knowing why, felt trapped. He no longer wanted to see the boy. He wanted to get out of there!

"Yeah, sure, sure, but I only got a minute," Les said. The woman pushed back the curtain for him to enter the bedroom. Les had to duck his head to go through the doorway.

Billy looked different than he remembered him. He always was a skinny runt of a kid, but lying in bed the boy seemed lost under the thin blankets.

Billy's face lit with pleasure. He struggled to sit upright in the bed.

"Hi, Les! Gee, it's swell of you to come over and see me."

"Should have done it a long time ago," Les said.

"Les, if Dad puts a hoop up on the coal shed would you teach me to play basketball? Huh, would you, huh?"

"Sure, sure thing, Billy. When the weather warms up, okay?"

"Gee, that's great. I want to play as good as you do. I'll bet I never do, though. I have Dad go to all the home games so he can tell me how you and the team do. But I'm mostly interested in you."

This frank praise was more than Les expected. He looked again at the thin body of the sick boy, and he felt almost ashamed he himself was so big and healthy in comparison. Les couldn't think of anything to say.

"We're awful proud of you, Les, living in the same neighborhood with you and all. I want to be just like you, Les. Just like you," the boy said. His eyes were bright, and the pale face had flushed from his excitement.

"You'll be better, Billy," Les said. He patted the tumbled brown hair awkwardly and backed blindly from the room. He heard both Hiltons crying softly.

Ernie laid a hand on Les's shoulder. He lowered his voice.

"The doctor just told us tonight that Billy will never walk again."

Les waved in the direction of the bedroom.

"But—but he thinks he's going to play basketball. You heard him in there."

"We haven't told him yet. We don't know how to say it." Ernie's voice broke, but he caught his lower lip in his teeth and controlled himself. Like he had learned to take hard luck.

Les was too stunned to make a reply. He hadn't dreamed of anything like this!

"Les, you're his hero. He keeps your scoring average. When they broadcast the games, mostly away from home, he listens on the little radio the doctor gave him. Les, that kid thinks you're just about it."

Ernie's hand seemed to burn on his shoulder. The man took it away, but Les thought he could still feel the weight there.

Les looked vacantly at the man, his thoughts busily churning on his own problem. It wasn't as simple as it had once seemed. He had thought only in terms of himself. Now there was Billy to think about. No, not

Billy, really—kids like Billy. Kids who hero-worshiped guys like himself whether he was deserving or not. Kids in other Shacktowns in other cities.

He pulled the door open with a jerk. He wanted to shut out the sight of that room—of Billy—of the whole world.

"Good night, Ernie," Les said.

As Les legged it through the big vacant lot between the Hiltons' and his own house, he argued bitterly with himself. Why had he stopped at the Hiltons' to-night of all nights? It just complicated things. He could look after himself, make his own decisions. What kind of a heel was he? How many Billy Hiltons were there? Kids who had a simple faith that everything was on the up and up, kids who made heroes out of guys like himself? Once again he was reminded of the freckle-faced boy who had stopped him outside the gymnasium that night. There were always kids hanging around the gym. Why couldn't they wait? They'd have their day. But that wasn't fair. No, they *should* be there, if basketball was to remain a boy's game. They were tomorrow's players, tomorrow's heroes. They deserved their chance.

He stopped by the house long enough to tell his dad he was going over to Jim Raines's house. And as he walked he knew everything was okay.

Luckily he caught Jim Raines as he was leaving the house to take in a movie with his wife. When the coach began to catch the drift of what Les was telling him, he pulled Les into the house. His wife looked at Les anxiously, but smiled reassuringly.

Les had spoken rapidly, getting a little mixed up, but he had to get it off his mind. Had to—before he had a chance to reconsider. He didn't spare himself.

"Les, I appreciate your honesty about these things. What are you going to do now?"

Les leaped to his feet and began to pace the room. Yeah, what could he do? Then it came to him. He leaned over the coach excitedly. He laughed crazily as the idea began to grow and become a part of him.

"Do? I'm going to play Billy Hilton's basketball for him! And he's going to be proud of me, because I'm not going to let him down!"

Raines grinned and got to his feet. The coach put a hand on his shoulder and gripped it warmly.

"Les, it will make the difference of being a good basketball player or a great ballplayer. I think you have it in you. There's a point or two to clear up yet." The coach frowned and went to the telephone.

"What are you going to do?" Les asked.

"I'm going to call the athletic commissioner. That will clear you. But, I'm afraid Fred Owens is going to make it tough on you when he finds out we've reported this. It might get him into hot water, you know."

"I'm not afraid of Fred. Go ahead, place that call."

"Those fellows don't play by referees' rules, Les."

The three of them exchanged glances. Les nodded at the telephone. Martha Raines slipped an arm over his shoulder as they stood there and waited for the coach to contact the long distance operator.

CHAPTER NINETEEN

THURSDAY AFTERNOON BEFORE PRACTICE
Coach Raines told the boys to sit down on the
bleacher seats. He wanted to talk to them. Les knew
he was the only one who suspected what it was all
about. The coach didn't waste any time getting to the
point.

"Boys, Les was approached by a gambler. You
know what that means. You can't bury a secret in a
small town, but I wanted you boys to get the straight
of it before you heard anything down on the square.
Les turned down the proposition and reported it to
me. I called the athletic commissioner. Les is in the
clear as far as the high school athletic commissioner is
concerned, but he might be in for some trouble from
other sources."

Les felt all eyes turn on him. Rip Castner spoke up.
"We're with you, Les!"

Others chorused the same remark. Les dropped his
eyes in embarrassment as he thought about things
they didn't know.

Raines kept his voice emotionless as he talked. He
mentioned how gamblers played upon a boy's pride
even while laying plans which would tear away his
decency. He didn't sermonize. He talked straight out
from the shoulder.

"Don't do business with any of these shady charac-
ters. Don't tell them, or anyone else, for that matter,
about the boys on the team, how they feel, personal

differences they might have or what plans we might
have. They use that information.

"Not only that, but innocent people sometimes talk
too much if they know personal things about the team.
It has to be a 'one for all, and an all for one' proposition on a basketball team. Stick closer together than
adhesive tape. There's one good thing that has come
out of all this."

"What's that?" Larry Ryan asked.

"It shows that some people think we might be going
somewhere this season. Now if you boys would get
the same idea we just might get the job done."

"Let's show 'em!" Rip Castner leaped to his feet.

Oddly enough, the gambling episode strengthened
the team. Les was surprised, and more than a little
discomforted, to find that the boys regarded him as
some kind of a hero. He felt far from it.

In absolute contrast to the heartbreaking string of
losses absorbed by the Raisner five, they squeaked
through three tight games against teams that should
have laid the hammer to them. Raines said it was their
team play. Maybe he was right. It was fun to be
playing on a hard-hitting balanced unit where everyone had a job to get done and contribute to the common cause. Whatever it was, their victory string had
been extended to a more impressive ten wins against
four losses.

Only four games remained on the season's schedule
until the sectional tournament got under way. Basketball fever gripped the town. The people began to take
a particular pride in noting Raisner's name mentioned
in the big city papers. Maybe a sectional winner
wasn't too much to expect.

When Les broke the ten-year-old fieldhouse scoring
record with a hot thirty-nine points, to better the old
one by nine points, businessmen began to call him by
name when they saw him on the square. Elmer
Robbins kidded Les that his grocery trade had in-

creased with a spurt because he had a basketball star working for him.

True, a few die-hards had been insulting when Les had scored but twelve points against Finley, but there were other fans who appreciated his rebounding and defensive floor play enough to go out of their way to tell him about it.

George Carney, the local sports writer, kept playing up the team as a unit in his column. It was "the team" this and "the team" that, and it helped shape the direction of the townspeople's conversation without their knowing it.

When Jim Raines locked the gym for closed practice sessions it seemed mysterious and exciting to talk about.

Les, sitting on the bench one afternoon in practice, overheard a conversation between the varsity coach and his assistant, Tom Williams. He knew it wasn't for his ears, but he was sitting so close to them he couldn't help but hear what they said.

"Jim, I have a hunch we're going to cop that sectional this year." Williams slapped Raines on the back in friendly banter. Raines winced under the blow, but he was growling with a smile on his face. Nevertheless, he ducked another wide swing and stepped out to the side lines to watch practice more closely.

"Let me live long enough to see it," Raines threw back over his shoulder.

"Listen, you have one of the sweetest guard combinations in high school basketball, and you know it. They're aggressive, and they can hit. Beach is the best rebounder in the state, and I wouldn't be surprised if he isn't by far the trickiest ball handler."

"They do all right," Raines tried to sound casual, but Les saw him swing a pleased look in his general direction.

"Now look at that sappy expression on Les's face, Tom. You have the kid thinking he's an All-Star,"

Raines said. It made him feel good inside. His improved playing had been a frequent topic of conversation between the varsity coach and himself. Raines wanted him to know he was doing all right for Billy Hilton.

On the other hand, things weren't going too smoothly between Judy and himself. The more he concentrated on basketball the less he saw of her. She voiced resentment against the game, adding her sentiments to those of the other girls who were being ignored by members of the team.

"When are they going to breathe for you boys?" Judy flashed on one occasion. Even that hadn't been as bad as the time he had told her they were starting a training table in the cafeteria and wouldn't be down at the gym on noon hours to dance.

Les began to worry when he saw other fellows escorting Judy through the halls between classes, but he shrugged it off. But he hadn't taken it so lightly until Doctor Merrill had laughingly told him that his picture still occupied the place of prominence in her room.

When Judy did encounter Les, he was in the library reading one of the newer books. He saw she was craning her neck to get a look at the title. She plunked her books on the table, hoping to get his attention, he knew, but he purposely kept his eyes on the book.

"Since when did you become the strong silent type?" Judy said.

Les grinned and put the book face down. He was learning how to handle girls, he told himself with pride.

"I haven't seen you around lately," Les said. He kept his tone casual and he was amused to watch her sputter.

"Of all the conceited nerve! I'm getting away from here!"

"Aw, sit down and cool off," Les said.

"Cool off! You should talk!" She sat down.

They regarded each other for a moment. Then both laughed.

"What are you reading?"

"It's a biography about George Washington Carver. You know, the guy who found so many uses for the common peanut."

"What's so interesting about that?"

"Listen, Judy, no kidding, you ought to read this book. Remember how I pitied myself, thinking all the breaks were against me? Well, this Carver guy wasn't only born in a shack, but he was born as a Negro slave. That's a pretty tough start, you know. Gee, and all the things that guy did for science!"

"Maybe I will read it," Judy said.

"Miss Garr gave it to me."

"I can rest assured it's the best of reading if Miss Garr recommended it," Judy said with sarcasm.

"Hey, you have Miss Garr all wrong, Judy. She's really a pretty swell person."

Judy looked at him thoughtfully. A tiny smile was on her face.

"What is there about you that makes people want to help you?"

"Huh? Maybe it's because I'm such a darned nice guy," Les said. He was laughing as Judy made a face at him. Then Judy became serious.

"You know, you have changed a lot, Les," she said.

"Is that good?"

"I think it's very good," Judy answered.

"If I have, and I know I've been trying pretty hard, Judy, I think it's because of basketball and the boys on the team."

Judy frowned as he mentioned basketball, but again she looked at him.

"How do you explain that?"

Les looked down at the table, not knowing how to put it into words. He thought of several things, but it embarrassed him to say it the way he meant it to sound.

"I don't know for sure. Maybe it's because for the first time in my life I feel I'm a part of something," Les said. That was it. He belonged. He was a team player. What he said next had no tie-in with his previous statement, yet it was very much a part of it in Les's mind.

"You know, Judy, we're going to win that sectional this year!"

CHAPTER TWENTY

THE MARSHALL TEAM CAME, WAS SEEN AND
was conquered by a seven point margin. It was far
from the Tomahawks' best played game. The shooting
average had fallen off to its lowest percentage of the
season. In fact, Marshall actually outscored Raisner
from the field. Fortunately, their shooting average was
also in the basement. The game was won merely because more foul shots had been hit from more foul
shots awarded to the Tomahawks.

The defensive playing was ragged in spots, but it
could easily be tightened. Les knew Raines had
placed so much emphasis on defensive playing, with a
green team on his hands, that he had almost ignored
offense. The coach had placed faith in the scoring
ability of his two guards.

It must have been like letting air out of air castles
for the coach when he watched his team suffer their
worst defeat of the season against a rugged Colby
team, 58 to 39. Of the 39 points, Les had contributed
21, Castner had made 9 but Ryan had slipped to a
scant 5. Rog Larking and Joe Taylor hadn't been able
to solve a shifting zone and had been held to a bare
basket each to show for their thirty-two minutes of
playing time.

Les wondered if the team had reached its peak.
Some teams played their best basketball at mid-season
and limped to a miserable showing by the tournament

play-off. Were the Tomahawks one of those teams?
What a time to slide downhill.

Eleven games won out of sixteen played wasn't a
bad season, Les had to admit, but if they lost the remaining two on the schedule, the story would be
different. Yet that would be a good season for Raisner
High School, which had concentrated more effort on
debating teams than it had on producing a serious
contender for a basketball title of any kind. But Les
wanted to play on a winner.

The boys had developed faster in one month than
most teams did in a season. Les had been amazed
when he realized these were the same players he had
called dubs before he reported for basketball. He was
proud that he had something to do with that improve-
ment.

Practice sessions lengthened. The street lights were
on long before the boys left the gym.

More than once the fast break threatened to become barnyard ball. Les was the only steady influence
to prevent complete catastrophe. He deliberately held
up the ball to slow them down when they got erratic.

Elbows flew and tempers flashed under the backboards. Yet through it all Les managed to keep his
temper in check. His good-natured remarks broke
more than one tense moment. His rebukes seemed to
slide in at the right times when more stern measures
were needed. More important, however, he had
played under Jim Raines before, and he anticipated
the need for quiet intervention among the boys when
they smarted most under the raging of the relentless
coach.

Raines drove himself and the boys almost to the
breaking point. Les knew the old man was thinking
tournament during every waking minute of the day.
Tom Williams hovered anxiously in the background,
but he didn't interfere.

When the Turner game rolled around Jim Raines

was at home in bed with flu. Tom Williams took over, hoping to win one for his fellow coach.

Williams was a milder person than Jim Raines, but he had a way of telling you, Les thought.

"Knuckle down out there. Each man play his position. Play it man to man," Williams said.

The team hadn't used the man to man defense much during the season, and Les wondered what Raines might have said if he had been there.

"Let's go!" Ryan said.

"Yeah, let's take 'em!" Larking joined in.

The team took the floor. Turner was still downstairs in the locker room. The Tomahawks could hear them yelling as they came up the steps. Then the Turner Eagles were also on the floor. One of their cheer leaders ran out to the center jump circle and placed a defiant stuffed eagle facing the Raisner fans.

Up above the scorekeeper's bench, the Turner radio broadcasting crew was making last minute checks on its equipment. The gymnasium public address system droned the players' names and numbers. Each school cheering section of students applauded at each name.

Castner lost the tip, and a Turner guard gained possession of the ball. Les pressed him, but the guard passed to a teammate who had anchored himself on the same side of the center stripe. The ball was moved up from the back court. Then the Eagles went into a deliberate delaying game, passing only when necessary and always out on the court.

Minutes ticked by and the Tomahawks began to get uneasy.

"Hold it!" Les yelled as Larking started to pull himself out of defensive position. Les waved him back. Rog wiped his hands on his trunks and licked his lips. The forward shifted his feet in place, not knowing what to do, but he cast a quick look at Les for reassurance.

Les was determined to get the ball. It might mean a

foul, but he tensed himself for an opportune moment. His eyes moved with the ball. He shifted his weight on his feet. Now!

Les lunged across the few feet that separated him from the Turner player who was about to receive the pass. The boy turned his hips toward him to shield the ball, but Les hooked it out of his hand and started down the floor. The referee's whistle stopped him before he got to the offensive foul circle.

The foul was awarded to Raisner! It was a one in one, and Les sank the first shot. Turner called time. Both teams trotted to their benches with the crowd's awakened roars in their ears.

Williams chewed his gum vigorously, plainly showing his excitement.

"Shift to the zone, but make sure that backboard is covered for a down-center drive. Les, move in for Taylor at forward. Joe, watch that number 29, he's tricky. Wait them out. If they want to stall, let them, but don't get rash."

Williams shoved them back on the floor and sat down. His eyes snapped in time to his fast-moving jaw. This was the assistant coach's first shot at a varsity game. He wanted to win it.

Les had two fouls called against him as he attempted to block the center when Rip let him slip through.

"Watch that, Rip. A truck could park in there," Les said.

Rip didn't make any comment, but Les could see the worried lines on his face. On the next play, Castner remained stationary and had a shot awarded him from a charging penalty against the Turner center.

The first half was almost a nightmare to Les as he yelled positions to his teammates. The Turner style had them baffled. They moved as though in a daze, and Les began to use sharper tones. The Tomahawks were aroused enough to hold the Eagles to a three point difference. The Eagles went downstairs leading 15 to 12.

Tom Williams shuffled through his scouting notes. His concern, so evident, would have been comical to see if circumstances had been different.

"I can't understand it. Turner hasn't played that kind of a game yet this season. Looks like they're trying out their tournament style on us."

"They play in the Shelbyville sectional, don't they?"

"Yeah, so don't get excited about it. We're going to find a way to beat them now. They're steady players, and they can be plenty fast if they have to be," Williams said. He looked from player to player, measuring each appraisingly. His eyes stopped on Les.

"Beach, when we get into the lead, I want you to stall as much as you can." Williams swung his eyes around to include the others.

"That means you guys are going to have to hustle. Run that ball when you get it, but don't think you have to shoot just to get rid of it. We need points. Castner, you're doing better in the keyhole; but Taylor, you're playing out too far. Be ready to follow up those shots."

Williams clapped his hands explosively.

"On your feet. You've had plenty of rest out on the floor. Talk it up out there; it sounds like a cemetery."

The second half started with more speed. Castner outjumped the Turner center and Ryan got the ball but was tied up. The Turner player got the tip but Taylor grabbed it to give the Tomahawks possession. Joe dribbled down the side line, almost stepping out of bounds as he dodged an opposing player. He cut across the keyhole, stopped too soon, wavered awkwardly but caught his balance. For a moment he was in the clear, but by the time he had made up his mind to shoot the ball was batted out of bounds.

Les took the ball from the referee and began to

weave from the waist up. His bounce pass went to Larking, but Rog passed back to Ryan.

Les tensed under the backboard as Larry arched his shot into the air. The ball dropped cleanly through the hoop.

Les signaled the press as Ryan came into deep court for a possible rebound. Both of them took a man, and the ball was trapped from the pass-in. Les once more passed to Ryan.

Larry overdrove the basket with a Turner player on his heels, but he hooked a left-hander back over his head. The ball circled the rim and came out, but Les was there tipping it for control. Both Turner players were now rebounding against Les, but each time Les kept the ball bounding against the backboard. Finally, Les managed to angle the ball through the hoop. Raisner was in the lead, 16 to 15!

The Eagles looked toward the bench and received some kind of a signal from their coach. Again they slipped back into the possession game.

The third quarter moved slowly for the restless fans. The delaying tactics employed by the Turner Eagles did not make a spectators' game. Yet a quiet tension prevailed.

Turner scored. Raisner matched the basket. Turner scored but Raisner once more retaliated with another basket, preserving their slender one point lead, 20 to 19.

The fourth quarter began. The Eagle players were looking at their coach, but he shook his head. Their delaying tactics continued. There were longer intervals between scores by either team. Then Roger Larking hit one of his favorite set shots from the corner, pulling the Tomahawks into a three point lead. Ryan unleashed a long one from the center of the floor. He shouldn't have shot because the board was unprotected, but the ball plunked through the hoop. The score mounted to a five point advantage: Raisner 24, Turner 19.

The Turner coach called time. Some of the Eagle fans were beginning to complain about the unprofitable stalling tactics.

Tom Williams motioned to Ralph Watts for faster action with the towels. He glanced up at the clock before bending down to talk to the boys.

"Okay, Les, do your stuff. There's less than three and a half minutes left to this ball game. Be careful of fouls yourselves. If you have a three point advantage in the last ten seconds, let them score. Take all the time you can before making that pass-in. If any of you boys see Les is going to be tied up, help him out. And Les, if we unbalance the court, pass off for a gift basket. Okay, let's go!"

Turner made the pass-in, wary of Les's side of the court. Ryan cut diagonally across the floor and stopped in front of the ball handler before he reached the ten-second line. Les was moving up fast from behind, casting a look over his shoulder to keep his man's position in mind.

Les leaped into the air to grab the Turner pass. Immediately, he wheeled around and dodged the oncoming Eagle player. The Turner guard backpedaled to keep in front of Les.

Les dribbled in place, his elbow held close to his side. He crouched low over the ball, but his eyes watched the Turner player. Les faked with his shoulders and moved around the player, but the back court had now filled with the black and orange Eagle uniforms. He circled back out, dribbling backward now. The bright uniforms of the Turner players made it easier to keep track of them.

Two men advanced cautiously toward Les. Les slowed the low bounce of the ball with his fingertips and waited. Then he began to dribble along the cen-

ter line, barely inside the offensive court. The temptation was too much for the Eagles. They began to
crowd him, hoping he would step over the line, but he
slipped away from them.

Les drove down the side line but reversed and cut
back out for less crowded territory. Another Turner
player joined the chase. The three players tried to
hem him in, but once more his fast footwork and body
fakes took him out of danger.

Fans were on their feet and yelling hoarsely as the
hysteria of the closing minutes of the game ticked off
on the relentless clock.

Turner players, knowing they had to get the ball if
they were to have an outside chance of pulling the
game out of the fire, swarmed around Les.

Les went down on one knee, still dribbling, looking
for an opening among the surrounding legs. His pass
snaked through the tangle. It was too low, but Taylor
scooped it up and quickly passed to Larking who was
standing alone under the backboard. With a deaden-
ing calm, Roger banked it in with a slight flick of his
wrist.

To everyone's amazement, the Tomahawks remained in position and let Turner score. Then the
team trotted slowly downcourt for the pass-in.

Castner was still smacking the ball against his
hands when the gun exploded to end the game. Time
had run out for the Eagles!

CHAPTER TWENTY-ONE

RAINES WAS BACK AT SCHOOL MONDAY. HE
was still weak on his feet, but he was so driven to
produce for the tournament no one could have forced
him to stay at home. He did begin to ease up on the
practice to the extent that he spent more time at
the blackboard diagraming offensive plays.

Les and the boys walked through the newer plays
several times before attempting to execute them at
game speed. Most of them were easy to pick up as
they were little more than modifications of the plays
they had been using during the season.

By Wednesday the pace had picked up. On Thursday afternoon Raines held a formal practice session,
which was unusual for him the night before a game.
The coach paced the floor, calling out changes in positions or yelling impatiently when someone would lag
behind too much for his liking.

The practice was concluded by a tapering off pro-
cess which left the boys breathing easily. When they
went for their showers, Raines followed them into the
locker room. He took a seat on the bench by the door
and waited for them to get dressed.

The boys who weren't quite dressed by the time
Raines began to talk listened as they buttoned shirts
or slipped on their shoes. The touch of nostalgia for
past games played was unmistakable in the coach's
voice. He talked about games he had seen, games he
had coached in the past—of dreams he'd had as a

young coach wanting to set the basketball courts ablaze with his teams.

Silently they listened. Some of that nostalgia, some of the traditions and some of the hopes rubbed off on them as they listened to their coach. Raines's voice whispered dreamily as he talked about them.

"Of all the teams, boys, you're the best I've had. There's still a lot to look forward to and I really haven't much reason to look back into the past, except there were some nice kids on those teams, kids like yourselves. Kids that gave it all they had, whether the score was in their favor or not. They had the will to win. I think you kids have it."

Les could feel his heart pounding in suppressed excitement. He wondered if others were aware of the building tensions. He looked around him, and he knew his emotions were shared by the others. He could tell by the determination mirrored in their eyes —the desire to win. Then the eyes began to shift around the room, eyes that wondered, as he had wondered, how it was affecting the others. Then those eyes swung their focus back to Jim Raines, whose voice had begun to rise in his excitement. The coach got up from the bench and walked back and forth, poking one or two of them in the ribs as he passed. Then he whirled around, his eyes afire as he brought his fist crashing into the palm of his hand.

"Beat Blake tomorrow night! Let the record books show a 13-5 season. It's a good record. Sure, there are some better, but it's still a good record."

The small locker room reverberated with the yells that broke out. The boys surrounded the old man and pounded him on the back in their outburst of excitement. His face was grinning widely as he hunched his shoulders. Yet Les thought he saw a suspicion of moisture in the old man's eyes. He was a sentimental guy, that Raines.

The coach pushed them back.

"Take it out on Blake," he said.

Les and the boys trooped up the stairs. They laughed and yelled as they pushed each other up the steps. They all stopped to look at the big playing floor surrounded by the rectangular rows of empty seats. They were silent as they looked out across the brightly polished floor.

The last home game of the season had been played. The big gym would no longer resound to the vibrant yells of the fans for that season. Well, the win over Turner had been a great climax to an almost ended season.

Les knew an emptiness was settling somewhere within him as he looked at the backboards, the foul lanes, the top of the keyhole and the center jump circle. He had played many hours on that floor. Now it was ended. He couldn't hold back a slight smile as he remembered the days when he had been barely able to get the ball up to the hoop, slinging it sideways with both hands. What a difference a few years could make.

Rip put his hand on Les's shoulder, almost as though he understood in some way the things Les was thinking about. Les draped his arm over the big center's shoulder in turn. Then Larry Ryan sneaked up between them and gave each a dig in their unprotected ribs.

Ryan let out a squawk as both of them took out after him. The shifty little guard dodged in and out among the other players who were sidestepping wildly as he dashed through them.

"Get that little runt!" Rip yelled.

Ted Haskell couldn't hold the slippery Ryan, who had hit the drop bar on the gym door and run outside. The boys split up and dodged in and out among the parked cars, but Larry managed to keep away until

Larking and Bob Gray converged on him from around the building. Ryan threw up his hands and ducked back between the cars, still jibing them.

Les saw the laundry truck swing into the drive, and he felt the breath catch in his throat.

"Larry! Watch out!"

The brakes of the truck squealed as the driver jammed on the emergency.

Les ran around the cars, fearful that he would see Ryan stretched out on the ground between the wheels.

Larry was leaning on the trunk of Joe Taylor's car, breathing heavily. His arms were trembling.

"You okay, Larry?" Les asked anxiously.

Ryan nodded his head without speaking. Then he straightened up with a sickly grin on his face.

"Whew! That was too close for comfort!"

The driver of the truck, seeing that the boy was unhurt, swore under his breath, something about the kids these days, and jerked the truck forward with a heavy foot on the accelerator.

The boys had lost their exuberance. They tried to hide their concern from the others, but in that moment, Les knew that the bonds that held this team went further than basketball games.

The next afternoon they climbed aboard the big silver bus in that same parking lot. Well-wishing fans had come down to the gym to see them off.

"Hey, you guys, look at this." Paul Sears called from the rear of the bus.

Les was amazed to see the caravan of cars which had pulled up behind the bus, bedecked in the crimson and white Raisner school colors. Sure, he and the fellows had seen a few cars before they had entered the bus, but now it was like cars stacked into a drive-in theater with a first-run movie. Horns blasted, beeped and blared periodically as they wound snake-like behind the bus on the highway.

The reserves set the tempo for the evening when they emerged with a healthy 65 to 49 win over the Blake Panther reserves.

Les opened the varsity game with a nice mid-court set shot. Castner poured two quick pivot hooks into the hoop to increase the lead. Ryan snagged a beauty from the side court, Larking got a lay-in and Taylor duplicated it with a drive from the other side. Everyone on the Tomahawk team had scored before the game was three minutes old. The scoreboard was blank for the home team while showing 12 big points for the Raisner five.

"Go get 'em, big team, go get 'em," the Raisner fans yelled, and the team did just that.

Coach Raines grinned happily from the bench when the Tomahawks came in. The Blake coach had called a time-out to talk to his players. As Les watched him, however, he was now screaming at them and jabbing his finger toward the Raisner team. Les grinned behind the towel he held to his face. He looked at his own coach who was hopping around with a different brand of excitement.

"You've got it! You've got it!" Raines was singsonging.

Les knew, as did the others, what the coach meant. The passing was clean, quick and efficient. There was no lost motion.

The half-time score was a brilliant 46 to 17. The third quarter ended 66 to 29. Although Raines substituted freely during the fourth quarter, the Crimson Tide poured in the points in a relentless barrage.

Blake Panther fans were almost thankful when the gun ended the slaughter 91 to 40.

The Tomahawks whooped in the showers. Blake was not regarded as a pushover by anyone. This just wasn't their night. The victory was a real scalp lock in their war bonnet. What a finale for a season!

George Carney, the sports writer for the Raisner paper, squeezed through the half-open door to congratulate the players and the coach. He read off the scoring credits he had copied from the official scorekeeper.

Les was surprised he had made 39 points during the game. Had he finally stopped his old habit of counting them while he was playing? He half-listened to the baloney the exuberant Carney was spouting. Going to take the sectional, going to take the regional, heck, maybe we're going to take the state; stuff along that line.

"Hey, Jim, I'll bet Crandell over at Appleton is doing the sweating now. Hey, what about that." Carney slapped the coach on the back.

Raines was watching Ralph Watts pick up castoff socks, supporters, shoes and jerseys. He wasn't paying too much attention to Carney either, Les mused.

"Sure, sure, but be careful what you write just the same."

"Boy, oh boy!" Carney babbled to anyone who would listen. He grabbed Jim Raines's shoulder to force the old man to listen.

"We've got a team!"

Raines finally gave him his attention. He paused a moment while looking at his players, then what he said he said in a proud voice meant for the boys.

"You bet we have a team!"

Les winked at Rip. They looked at the others. They knew how Jim Raines meant that statement. The boys laughed. Raines closed the door on Carney's heels and leaned back against it.

"Boy, that guy talks a mile a minute. Let's go tackle a steak." He opened the door again, nodding to each as they passed from the room.

Tom Williams took a last look and snapped out the light behind them. "All clear, Jim," he said.

CHAPTER TWENTY-TWO

LES WAS TALKING TO JUDY AT HER LOCKER when Rip Castner found him.

"C'mon, hurry up before we miss it," Rip exclaimed.

"Miss what?"

"Holy cow, they're giving the sectional pairings. There's a radio on down at Benson's office. Let's go!"

Les needed no further urging. He gave a quick "I'll be seeing you" wave of the hand to Judy and took off with Rip.

Most of the team members were already in the high school office. Their attention was riveted to the small radio on the clerk's desk. Sectional pairings were being announced in a trained, matter-of-fact voice, but Les knew the boys clustered around this radio and other radios in the state weren't taking it matter-of-factly.

Ryan snorted and stood up to relieve his back muscles.

"Good gravy, why don't they announce Appleton's sectional drawings! Appleton does start with an "A" doesn't it?"

Tom Williams also stood up to straighten kinked muscles.

"They'll announce all the Indianapolis and Marion County teams first. They always do. Then they'll swing around picking out those sectionals where the state favorites will play," Williams said.

"That means us, then," Ryan said.

"Maybe we're not regarded very high," Rog Larking said. He laughed nervously.

"Yeah, but we'll show 'em different," Rip Castner boasted.

Ryan edged closer to the radio. He waved his hand downward.

"Hey, pipe down! A guy couldn't hear the commercials the way you guys yak."

"Who wants to hear 'em?"

Les watched the strain of excitement on the face of the varsity coach. Raines looked older and grayer to Les in that moment. Without knowing why, he moved to the old man's side. Raines put an arm around him and lowered his voice.

"This one is our last one, eh, Les boy?"

"I wish it were only our first," Les said. How he wished it could be. The coach's hand tightened on his shoulder in response.

"Hey! Here it is. Grab a pencil, one of you guys!"

At that moment the tardy bell rang. The boys looked up, startled. They knew they should be in classes. They looked at Mr. Benson, the principal, but he didn't say anything. He couldn't. He was too busy writing the sectional pairings. The boys grinned their relief and tried to hear the rest of the announcement.

"We drew a bye! We drew a bye! Hot dog! We drew a bye!" Ryan chanted.

"Shut up, for Pete sakes, shut up!" someone groaned as he frantically scribbled team names.

"Easy there, easy there," Raines said softly. His face was tight.

Mr. Benson straightened up from his writing and flicked the switch on the radio at the same time. He looked over the tops of his glasses at them until they quieted down.

"This is the way I have it. Appleton plays Colby in the first round. If they get by Colby, and some sports

writers, I noticed, pick Colby for the major tournament upset team, they play Bayfield. Let's see," the
principal held the paper up closer to his face, "before
we get into all that who plays who business, we'll look
at our own pairing.

"We play the Dinsfield team first. After winning
that one" (a loud cheer followed that calm statement), "we take on the winner of the Millford-Win-
inger game. Then, boys, we're in!"

"Both those teams have claws out for tournament
play," Raines said seriously.

"Aw, they're just little wide spots in the road like
us," Ryan said.

"Never underrate a team at tournament time,"
Raines warned solemnly.

Mr. Benson held up his hands to quiet their yelling.
The boys quieted down mostly because "Old Ben"
had been a good sport about everything.

"All right, boys, let's move along to classes now.
Good luck."

All through the day and the rest of the week the
boys heard the good wishes of their classmates. At the
pep session Raines thanked the students for their support throughout the season. He reminded them about
observing good sportsmanship and conduct throughout the tournament.

The cheer leaders put on a burial skit for the opposing teams. Balloons had been painted in opposing
school colors, and a hidden student popped each one
as the knell of doom was read solemnly by one of the
cheer leaders. Then a huge red and white balloon shot
up toward the gym rafters with a big Tomahawk
painted on it. The students picked up the Raisner war
chant in loud and proud voices. Again Jim Raines was
called upon to speak.

The coach introduced the players and asked them
to stand in place. He said something nice about each

one of them, although he made sly comments about them which brought gales of laughter from the students who knew them the best.

"Rip Castner's sole object in winning the sectional, so he tells me, is to release three hundred and twelve students from bondage for the one-day vacation the school board has promised should we win."

Rip blushed and looked owlishly from side to side.

"Seriously," Raines continued, "we're counting a lot on Castner. He's developed fast this season, and we'll need that hook shot of his many times, I suspect. Rip is a junior and will be back with us for another season.

"Next to Rip is a little peewee that has the knack of getting in the right place at the right time. Stand up, Larry. Ryan is a good shot, a steady ball handler and has two more years with us, being only a sophomore. He will be a dangerous opponent for any school. He's also the practical joker on the team.

"Next to Ryan is Joe Taylor. Joe is one of the two seniors on the team. We wish Joe could be with us next season. He didn't come out for basketball until last year, and we wish he had started sooner. I suspect one of the small colleges will be more than happy to add Joe to their playing roster. He's quiet, dependable and a good team player. We have a hard time getting Joe to shoot, but as you know from past games, when Joe fires the scoreboard usually blinks.

"Roger Larking is the other forward. He's a speed merchant, also holding the conference hundred-yard dash record, I understand. Earlier this year he sprained his ankle in football, but he recovered in ample time for basketball season, I'm glad to say. Rog is a good shot and a good team player. In fact, all of these boys are good team players. I think that's an outstanding thing about them. Rog gets a little excited sometimes, especially when we're behind. But he puts out that old spirit and helps us bounce back.

"The last player on the starting team is also the act-

ing floor captain. Les Beach. I think that Les has overcome a lot of difficulties to emerge the fine team player and true competitor that he is. We depend upon
Les for rebounds and defensive strategy. He's the
playmaker. He also hold the school single game scoring record. He's had all our hearts in our mouths when
he goes into the stall that helps put the game on ice
for us. Les is definitely college material. I'm sorry
we're going to lose him this June, but I think we'll
hear more about him in the sports columns when he
gets to college."

Johnny Kerr, Paul Sears, Ted Haskell, and Bob
Gray were also introduced. Raines spoke highly of
them, commenting they were just as important a part
of the team as were the starters. Most of them had
two years yet to play before they graduated.

The boys on the team sat down again. They bent
their heads as their fellow students paid homage to
them with rafter-shaking yells.

CHAPTER TWENTY-THREE

THE RAISNER TEAM SAT TOGETHER IN THE big Appleton gym to watch the host team of the tournament take on their first opponent.

"I hope Appleton comes through," Rip Castner commented.

Roger Larking jerked up his head in surprise.

"Why?"

Rip shrugged, but kept his eyes on the playing floor.

"Oh, I don't know. It'd be more fun to beat an outfit like that than some team that was playing on inspiration only."

"What if we're the team playing on inspiration only?" Les asked.

Rip set his jaw defensively.

"Well, that's different!"

Bob Gray slapped Castner on the shoulder and laughed.

"Yeah, that's different! They're them, and we're us!"

The other boys joined in the laughter and roughed Castner with sly digs of elbows and hearty backslaps.

Rip flushed as Ryan's elbow found a vulnerable spot. He whirled around, some of the good nature fading from his face.

"Hey, lay off, you guys!"

Larry Ryan leaped down a seat row as he dodged a wild right.

"Temper, temper, temper," the little guard said.

"Cut it out," Rip said in a huffy tone.

"You can do better than that under the backboard," Ryan answered, but he kept his distance from the tall center.

Some of the Appleton fans turned to frown at the noise makers behind them. One of them voiced his displeasure openly.

"Is that all you Raisner guys can do, make noise?"

A friend of his encouraged him.

"You tell 'em."

"Yeah, you tell 'em," others chorused, but they swung their attention back to the game.

Paul Sears spotted Jim Raines and Tom Williams coming up the bleacher steps, and he tapped Les on the arm in a quick signal. Les passed the signal on.

By the time the varsity coach and his assistant had sat down, the Raisner team was a model of tranquillity. Someone blurted a giggle and others joined in, which made Raines and Williams cast a reprimanding look in their direction.

"Can the horseplay, boys. You're up here supposedly learning what you can about the man you might be guarding later in the tournament. That means Appleton."

All of Raines's remarks the last few days were slanted as though there was no doubt in his mind which team would be facing them in that final game.

Colby tried to live up to the sports writers' predictions of being a dark horse team. Entering the tournament with everything to gain and nothing to lose by way of reputation, the Colby team was playing without the pressure which rode the shoulders of last year's regional winners.

The score remained even, one team scoring only to be matched by the other. It was fast-break basketball all the way, and Les knew Crandell, the Appleton coach, had hoped to use his first team sparingly. The resistance of the Colby team had changed those plans in a hurry. If the Appleton Tigers were to stay in the tournament, they had to subdue a stubborn team in this opener.

Jim Raines was delighted, and he made no effort to conceal it.

Les watched Sage of Appleton pull the game out of the fire for his team with a three point basket—an awarded foul and a lay-in. The Appleton team dragged its heels off the floor with a 63 to 60 win.

Tom Williams said something about getting the breaks, and Les agreed with him. He couldn't help but think that as of almost that precise moment, sixty-four teams in the state had now been eliminated.

The next game was uneventful, and after watching the first half the boys headed for the automobiles to travel back to Raisner. It looked as though Needley would be an easy victor, and the next morning's paper substantiated that belief.

Thursday evening found the boys back in the Appleton gym, as avid as any of the spectators there. Grins were brought to their faces when some of the Appleton crowd caught sight of them and led a yell against them. Of course, Appleton wasn't playing, but that made little difference. A few of the defeated Colby supporters led an impromptu cheer for Raisner, and the boys watched some of the Raisner fans acknowledge the yell with a "Thank you Colby, Colby, we say thank you!"

Coach Raines, Tom Williams and Doctor Merrill drove the boys down to Appleton Friday morning to check them in at the Graybank hotel.

Raines lingered behind the others to give them final instructions.

"If there's a radio in your room, you can listen to that, but I prefer you to get a nap. Relax as much as you can. Williams and the Doc and I want to catch a little of the first game, but we'll give you a buzz or send Ralph Watts after you so you can get to the gym in time to dress. It'll only take you a minute or two to get to the gym from here. See you later."

The boys leaned against the room clerk's desk and asked for their keys. As the clerk gave the keys to them, he regarded them with a worried frown. Unconsciously he looked at a big sectional pairing poster behind him.

"Better scratch Appleton right now," Rip drawled.

"Huh, you might come crawling back here this afternoon," the clerk retorted with spirit.

"Wishful thinking," Rip said as he juggled his key in his hand.

Les saw the magazine rack across the lobby and headed for it.

"Hey, Rip, as long as we're going to be cooped up for a while, I think I'll get a magazine to read," Les said.

"Don't get the wanderlust, Les boy. I thought I caught a glimpse of Judy a minute ago," Rip said with a frown on his face. He took a step as though to follow his teammate.

Les, watching him, shook his head.

"You're getting like a doting uncle, Rip. It's nothing like that. I just want to get a magazine, that's all. Holy cow, you can even pick the magazine out for me, if you want."

"Aw, c'mon Castner, let's go up to the room," Ryan said, making the elevator operator wait for the lanky center.

The elevator doors had barely closed when Les became aware of heavy cigar smoke behind him.

"Okay, Les, take a little walk!" a familiar voice said in his ear.

Les took his time turning around. He knew who it was.

"What's on your mind, Fred?" he said.

"You'll soon see, punk. Spilled the beans, didn't ya?

Made it hot for me with certain guys, didn't ya? Get moving!" Owens gave Les a hard-handed shove between the shoulder blades. Les stumbled forward a step. It wasn't the shove that bothered Les. He didn't have much doubt that he could whip the pudgy Owens. It was the small, round, hard steel he could feel probing into him.

Les tried to be casual. There was no telling how far Fred might carry this thing. Les wanted to yell and dash down the street, but something restrained him. It wasn't fear, really, but more like stubborn pride.

"You always were a nervy cuss," Fred admitted almost reluctantly. "Just keep on walking, Les, you're doing fine. Here, turn here at the corner into the alley. I got a couple of friends waiting for me."

As Les walked into the alley ahead of the gambler, he weighed that last remark. How many were "a couple"? His eyes darted from side to side, looking for avenues of escape. He gauged the height of the board fence to the right of him and tried to count out to himself how long it would take him to scale it.

He almost took the first step when someone emerged from a garage doorway to block his path. Actually, there were two men, Les discovered as a smaller one stepped from behind his bulky companion.

"Is this the kid?" the bigger one asked. His face was unshaven and dirty. His smaller companion sidled up to Les and rammed a hard elbow into the basketball player's ribs.

The man's weasel-like face twisted with convulsive twitches.

"Like some more of that, big boy?"

"You'll need some help," Les snapped hotly.

The smaller man's lips drew back in anger.

Les tightened his stomach muscles as the sharp elbow hit him again. It had been higher this time and slid off his ribs. A pain shot through his chest. He started forward, but the big man thrust himself in his path.

The unshaven man shoved his companion aside rudely and pinned Les's arms behind his back in an iron grip. Les surged against the hold without success. The big man's laugh rasped against his ears.

"Watcha want done with the kid, Fred?"

The man almost jerked Les off his feet as Les continued to struggle in his bearlike grasp. The man began to pant from his exertions. Les could smell the stale cigarette breath blowing in hot spurts against the back of his neck.

Fred Owens slapped him sharply across the face, and Les stopped trying to get away. He was trembling with anger. His eyes blazed at Owens, and the fat man took a backward step.

"Listen, Les, you already cost me money, and not a little trouble. You fooled me. I thought you might get it in your crazy head to pitch a few games away, but you didn't. That cost me. My original idea was just to hold you until the tournament is over. You give us any more trouble and I'll have Charlie clobber you. Understand?"

Owens thrust his heavy-jowled face close to Les, and it infuriated the man that he couldn't hold his gaze steady against those blazing eyes.

"Yank him into this garage so we won't attract any attention. One yip out of you, Les, and we'll conk you. Now get moving."

It took several minutes before they could manipulate Les into the garage. Dutchie, the smaller man, tried to close the garage doors, but Les almost knocked him down as he was crashed into the heavy double doors by the struggling Charlie. Fred Owens danced around them, yelling directions. Then he closed his mouth grimly and chopped at Les with a short piece of two-by-four he had found in the garage.

The light admitted by the small dust and cobweb

covered window was feeble and unencouraging. Les felt his hopes sink as he ceased to struggle. His arms ached from the tight hold, and he was having difficulty in breathing. His breath came in sobbing gasps.

"Now you're using some sense," Fred panted. He blotted at his fat face with a small silk handkerchief. Then he motioned to Dutchie with his free hand.

"Find something to tie the kid with. Charlie can't hold him forever."

Fred's eyes moved along the walls of the garage for a piece of rope or wire as Dutchie made a superficial search.

"I done told Charlie to bring something to tie the kid with, but he's so all-fired smart he didn't bring nothing," Dutchie said in a complaining voice.

Fred pointed overhead.

"There, what's that? Over there, above you, more to the left."

A piece of rope dangled from a torn tarpaulin.

Les spotted the rope before Dutchie did. Les quietly drew a deep breath, realizing it was now or never. Frantically, he lunged and twisted in Charlie's relaxed grasp. He kicked out with his feet, trying to crack a thin shinbone.

The man cursed, once more closing those big hairy arms around him. Les felt that smothering squeeze stop the breath in his throat. Every rib seemed to crack under the pressure. Fury, fear and desperation strengthened him to renewed effort. He felt himself slipping free.

"Halp, halp! Grab him! Grab him, I tell you!" The big man grabbed at empty air. For a moment his companions stood there, both looking startled in that frozen second.

Les sidestepped and put his weight behind an overhand right. His fist chopped into the unshaven face. The big man grunted and backed away.

Dutchie squealed as Les grabbed his shirt front. Again his hard balled fist smashed into a face. Les felt the teeth cutting into his hand as they were pushed back into the man's mouth. He shoved Dutchie into Charlie, and both lost their balance to fall to the floor.

Fred Owens tried to trip him as he struggled to open the door. Les turned viciously and swung in Fred's retreating direction. Owens bleated as a knuckle cut into his cheek.

Again Les struggled with the doors. His breath was jerky with his desperation. He threw a look over his shoulder and saw Charlie reaching for him. Les threw himself flat against the door, but Charlie managed to hook his fingers in Les's shirt collar. Les strained forward with all the drive he could muster in those muscular, basketball-conditioned legs. He heard the shirt material tear, the momentary release, and then he burst almost like an explosion from the garage into the alley.

"Get him! Get him!" he heard Fred Owens' fear-laden voice screaming from behind.

Without a backward glance, Les vaulted over the board fence and into a chicken yard. The chickens squawked as he lit in their midst, running crazily into the flimsy poultry netting on the other side of the small enclosure. Ignoring them, Les reached through the slats of the gate and unhooked the bent wire that held it. He dodged through the gate and locked it behind him.

He ran through the yard, between the houses and out onto the sidewalk. He slowed down and tried to walk so as not to attract attention to himself. He was aware of the chill of the early March air. Somewhere behind him, he couldn't remember where, he had lost his jacket. His face was scratched and stung against the wind. He swung his arms experimentally as he walked.

A woman, shaking a mop out on her front porch,

stared at him strangely. Someone in a passing car honked at him, but he kept going.

Les turned the corner and almost sagged with relief when he saw his father standing on the hotel steps. Sam was rolling a big cigar in his mouth, looking very expansive. Les had a crazy flash of his father trying to be a big shot.

As soon as his dad caught sight of him, however, the cigar dropped from his hand unnoticed. His father ran to his side and put an arm supportingly under Les's shoulder.

"Les, what happened? Good gravy, boy, you've been in one real scrap!" The man answered his own question as he peered anxiously into Les's eyes. "Your eyes are clear, that's good."

"Dad, help me up to my room and get Doctor Merrill. I think every rib must be broken."

CHAPTER TWENTY-FOUR

RIP CASTNER, WHO HAD BEEN SPRAWLED stomach down on the bed as he listened to the radio, scrambled to his feet when Sam Beach helped Les into the room.

"Good night! What happened to you?"

Instead of answering, Les sat down heavily on the edge of the bed.

Larry Ryan, who shared the hotel room with Rip and Les, came out of the shower stall with a bound when he heard Rip's explosive question. He stood there blankly with water dripping on the floor. His eyes bugged as he took in the scene.

"What's up?" Ryan asked.

Rip snatched up a clean towel and tossed it to Ryan by way of an answer.

"Here, stick this under the cold water and bring it back."

Larry padded barefoot into the shower and soaked the towel. He wrung it out and took it back to Rip, handing it to him silently.

"And here I thought Les had gone galloping off with Judy," Rip said self-accusingly as he bathed Les's face. He patted Les's face with the towel, trying to avoid the discolorations and cuts.

Les again opened his eyes when Rip removed the towel. He grimaced.

"My ribs kind of hurt. I don't know whether I've busted anything or not. Look, Rip, get Doctor Merrill, will you? Tell him to come up to the room. Say, wait a minute. Does Raines know I've been gone?"

A worried frown creased his forehead as he looked at his teammates.

"No, he and Williams ran into some old coaching buddies down in the lobby. Raines put in a telephone call to the rooms and asked about everybody before he went out. We told him everything was okay in room 612."

"Thanks, Rip," Les said.

Castner jerked his jacket off the back of the chair at the foot of the bed. He paused in the doorway to take another look back at his teammate. Les had stretched back on the bed and closed his eyes.

"I'll be back in a jiff. Maybe Doc Merrill is down in the coffee shop. I'll go see."

The tall center closed the door hurriedly but quietly behind him.

Les reopened his eyes to see Ryan hovering over him. The guard was now dressed except for his socks and shoes.

"What happened, Les?" he whispered.

When Les didn't answer immediately, Sam crooked his finger at Larry.

"I'll tell you what happened, and I wasn't even there. That Fred Owens had something to do with this. Ain't that right, Les?" His father swung his head around. Les merely nodded, but his dad continued in a more heated tone, "Fred said something to me a while back in Raisner, only I didn't connect together what he meant then, something about getting Les. I didn't say anything to Les, knowing he would get riled up about it and maybe do something he shouldn't."

Sam squeezed his powerful hands together and popped his knuckles.

"By golly, I'm going to get that monkey run out of Raisner."

They heard a key scratch in the lock and saw Rip open the door and stand aside for Doctor Merrill. Sam got up and gave the doctor his chair by the bed. He put his hand on Doctor Merrill's shoulder.

"Take good care of him, doc." The squat, thickset man's voice was husky.

"I'll do my best, Sam," the doctor said. He bent over Les.

His examination seemed almost too brief to Les and the onlookers. The fingers were light and skillful. The doctor's questions were unemotional and direct. Then he straightened, pursed his lips and leaned back in the chair.

Les sat upright in the bed and grabbed at the doctor's hand.

"Don't tell me I can't play! Don't tell me that!"

"Les, we have to be sensible. I'll tell you. I know Doctor Sage here in town. He has an X-ray machine. I'd feel better if we had a picture of those ribs, Les."

Rip Castner frowned at the doctor.

"Hey, there's a guy named Sage that plays on the Appleton team. Heck, his old man wouldn't do anything for us."

The doctor motioned to Les to get up. He put on his own overcoat. Then he put a hand on Castner's shoulder.

"Rip, our profession renders aid when and where it is needed. It will make no difference."

"Well, if you say so, but gee, isn't there some other doc we could take Les to in this burg?"

"Let's go," Les said quietly.

As they rode up in the elevator in the medical building, Les thought about Sage the basketball player. What would he think if he knew his dad had given help to his opponent? Funny, the way things turned out.

Doctor Sage was busy, the receptionist told them. Ryan glanced nervously at his watch and began to drum his fingers on the arm of the chair. When Rip flashed an irritated look at him, Larry barely tipped his head to indicate his watch.

The doctor's inner office door opened. He had an arm around his son, giving him some fatherly advice in tones deep with pride.

As the doctors exchanged greetings and Doctor Merrill stated the reason for their call, Bob Sage recognized Les for the first time.

"Hey, what's the matter with you?" His voice was puzzled but friendly.

"Nothing much, I hope." Les cracked a grin as he spoke. He didn't want to tell Bob Sage he was wondering if he had fractured a rib or two.

Bob read the fleeting distress in Les's eyes, but he didn't laugh.

"Beach, I've looked forward to playing against you in this tournament. Don't let anything happen that will change that, fellow."

"Thanks, Sage. I hope it hasn't already happened. You outplayed me the last time, and I want to even the score if I can."

Bob laughed and winked at Castner and Ryan, who weren't particularly in favor of this friendly exchange. They grinned weakly when Les gave them a sharp look.

"Dad, do the best you can for this guy. He's a real basketball player, even if he does play for the wrong school."

Bob Sage took Les's hand.

"See you in the final." Then Bob went out the door.

"Probably hurrying off to spread the glad tidings," Rip growled as he punched Larry forward to follow Les into Doctor Sage's office.

The two doctors half-crouched as they squinted at the drying X-ray. Les heard Doctor Merrill's sigh of relief, and he suddenly felt better.

"Tape that boy up and he'll be able to play, Bill," Doctor Sage said.

"We appreciate what you have done for us," Doctor Merrill said.

Doctor Sage waved his hand in the air, dismissing the idea that he had done much of anything. His eyes twinkled as he looked at Les.

"By golly, Beach, if Raisner beats Appleton, I'm going to have some explaining to do around town."

The doctor didn't sound worried.

"You can send the bill to the school, Harry," Merrill said conversationally as they prepared to leave.

"Let's just chalk this one up to better basketball and the boys who play the game. Good luck, son, but I hope you don't make a monkey out of my boy." Doctor Sage shook Les's hand. Les knew he was safe. Bob Sage could hold his own!

Jim Raines was running around the locker room like a crazy man when they reported to dress for the game.

"Good grief! What's the matter with you guys? Don't you realize we take the floor in about five minutes?"

The boys undressed quickly. Les stood with his arms held up for Doctor Merrill who was winding tape around him. That was almost too much for the gray-haired coach. He watched with disbelieving eyes. His voice was strained as he fought to control it.

"What happened to you? For gosh sakes, can't someone tell me what's going on in this madhouse?"

"Les got banged up pretty bad by Fred Owens and some others," Doctor Merrill said crisply. He tore strips of tape without looking up.

"I knew it! I knew it!" Then, realizing he was making a spectacle of himself, Raines just as quickly quieted down.

Uneasiness settled over the team members. Boys exchanged quick glances. They looked at Les, who was having his jersey slipped over his head by Rip and Larry.

"Gosh, that's tight," Les grunted. He rolled his shoulders experimentally and took a deep breath. He saw Raines watching him anxiously. Les faced the group. His eyes blazed with that old competitive fire they knew so well.

"Well, what are we waiting for? Let's go up and knock them off!"

Nervous grins broke out. Ryan started screeching and pounding backs. Yells broke out as the Tomahawks surged up the broad ramp.

The Raisner team was met by the happy yells of their fans as they took the floor. Cheer after cheer arose as each player took his turn at the lay-ups. Les was the only one to miss his shot.

He caught Raines's nod as he trotted to the center of the floor. Someone was with the coach, and Raines motioned to him to come to the bench.

Raines's voice was loaded with meaning as he introduced the man to the basketball player.

"Les, this is an old friend of mine, Bob Griggs. He's a basketball scout for a university. He came up here to watch you play."

Les was both elated and depressed. Here was a chance to go to college! That was what Raines meant. Yeah, and here he was taped up tighter than a drum. What a break, what a lousy break. Weren't things ever going to turn out right for him?

"I'll play the best I can, Mr. Raines," he said simply. There wasn't anything else to say.

The pride Raines had in him burst out in one glorious unguarded moment. The coach patted him encouragingly on the back.

"I know you will, Les. You're my kind of player. You play it all the way!"

Les trotted out to the west court and neatly took the

pass from Ryan, who had held up the ball when he had seen him coming. As his arms lifted to release the ball, Les felt a tug in his chest. The ball fell several feet short of the backboard. Ryan shook his head resignedly.

"Take it easy, Les, for gosh sakes, take it easy," Larry pleaded in a side whisper.

Les made an impatient motion and glanced at his other teammates.

"Don't worry about me. I'll be all right as soon as I get loosened up. It looks like some of the others better take it easy."

Ryan caught a pass from Castner and spun the ball with his fingertips without shooting.

"Huh? What do you mean by that?"

"Look at them sweat. They're in better condition than that."

"Aw, they're just nervous. That'll make you sweat. Look at me."

"Nuts. It's different. Larry, I'm no doctor, but I think those guys are coming down with something."

Larry flipped a one-hander at the hoop, but didn't follow it up.

"You're imagining things. C'mon, Raines will be pulling us in to find out what we're gabbing about."

Les shifted over until he was standing by Roger Larking. He could hear the forward's heavy breathing.

"What's wrong, Rog? Feeling a little low?"

"Yeah, I feel a little hot. Funny thing, just a moment ago I was griping about how cold it was in the gym. Even made a crack about how stingy Appleton was with their coal."

Les's eyes narrowed as he saw Larking's hand trembling before he caught the ball. Something was definitely wrong!

Joe Taylor wiped the perspiration from his forehead with the sleeve of his warm-up jacket before he took his next shot.

Ted Haskell stumbled on his lay-up. Ted's face had that flushed look. Paul Sears, who had followed up Haskell, was breathing too hard for the mild exercise he had been taking.

Les watched in puzzlement, but a growing fear was in his mind. He reached a decision. He motioned to the team with his hand and jerked his head for emphasis when they looked like they were going to ignore his summons. He was the acting team captain and they finally came from habit.

"What's the matter with you fellows? You look like you've been dragged through a knothole! Come on, guys, give. What's up?"

Paul Sears turned to take a shot. The others took their cue from Paul and began to pass the ball in an ever-enlarging circle. Les stepped into the circle and hooked the ball out of the air. The boys looked at him sheepishly. Les put the ball against his hip and singled out Rip Castner.

"What do you make of it, Rip?"

"How should I know?" Castner said peevishly.

"You're making too much out of nothing, Les. We're just coming down with one of those late winter colds," Paul Sears said.

"I think you guys are coming down with flu."

"Nuts, you aren't a doctor yet, Les," Paul grumbled.

"Hey, wait a minute," Rip put his hands on his hips and looked startled. "Rog, didn't you tell Larry and me you heaved your hash this afternoon?" Rip asked.

"Heck, they all look pukey, now that you've mentioned it," Larry said.

"Let's hope it isn't that bad." Les tried to sound cheerful.

"Boy, Raines keeps harping about there aren't any such things as breaks in a basketball game! What do you call this?" Castner said.

"An epidemic," Les said without humor in his voice. Ryan looked at Les.

"What are we going to do about it?"

"I'm thinking what Jim Raines would want, Larry. He would never willingly play a boy who was ill. All of you know that."

"But, Les, Rog and Joe are regular starters. We need them. We're going to need everyone on the team," Larry said with heat.

Rip Castner glanced around the loose circle of players. He tapped Les.

"Okay, Les, most of us, including yourself, have no business out on this floor right now. You make the decision with us, to play, or to tell Raines we're not able."

"It would break the old man's heart!" Johnny Kerr blurted in a scared voice.

Les looked from player to player. They met his eyes with that steely determination that had put them into the win column so many times during the season. They didn't look sick to Les now. Maybe he had been wrong.

"We play!" Les said.

The warning buzzer cleared the floor. Raisner had now entered the sectional!

CHAPTER TWENTY-FIVE

JIM RAINES TRIED TO GRAB THE HANDS
of all his players at once. His voice was choked with
strain and emotion.

"I don't have to tell you boys how much I want this
game. Go out and get it for me!"

"We'll get it for you. How about it, gang?" Les
yelled.

Rog Larking was unknowingly pressing into his side
and Les wanted to break away before the grimace on
his face became obvious to the keen-eyed Doctor Merrill.

The team broke from the coach in a surge of bright
crimson playing uniforms. Chatter swept from man to
man as they took their positions.

Castner's long reach barely commanded the tip
from the lanky Dinsfield center. Ryan was tied up immediately by an alert player. The referee brought the
ball back to the center circle for the jump.

Ryan crouched tensely, his eyes straining upward.
He went up almost with the ball. Although he was
shorter than the Dinsfield guard, he tapped the tip
back to Les.

For a moment it looked like Les was also going to
be tied up, but his elusive shift outmaneuvered his opponent. Changing hands, as he so often did, Les
spurted down the floor in alternate changes of pace.
The ball beat a rapid tattoo as he crouched over it. Almost stopping, he backpedaled, dropped the ball be-

hind him while dribbling and, again changing hands,
he brought the ball forward. As he cut across the
court for a lay-up, the Raisner fans leaped to their
feet, screaming hysterically. The tips of his fingers
were above the hoop when he gently released the ball.

Les felt something pull in his chest, and he stumbled when he hit the floor. He was out of bounds from
the momentum of his leap into the air, and he was
somewhat surprised when two strong arms caught him
to hold him erect. He never knew who it was, but he
remembered the encouragement in the man's voice.

"That's basketball! Go take 'em, kid!"

Raisner fans whooped as Les snatched the ball from
the Dinsfield end court pass-in. His quick shove pass
to Castner set up another two points.

The Dinsfield player looked disgusted with himself
as he passed the ball in again. He made sure he kept
the ball on the other side of the court from the black-
haired guard wearing the big 11. But little Ryan was
immediately behind the Dinsfield receiver, both arms
spread wide. The Dinsfield man tried to jump up and
hook a pass over his head, but Castner blocked the
ball with an outflung hand. It was a free ball, and
crimson uniforms dominated the white uniforms as
players fought for its possession.

Now Rip went down in a tangle as the players
knocked him off his feet. Les made a shallow belly
dive across the floor and brought the ball in under his
body. A shoe thumped into his side, and he involuntarily let go of the ball as the sharp pain made him
gasp.

The referee had both arms high in the air, and Les
knew it was a called toss. A Dinsfield player helped
him to his feet, but Les was so preoccupied with
where he was going to tip the ball that he forgot to
thank him.

Les went up into the air and captured the tip. The
ball went back to Joe Taylor, who was almost un-

guarded. Joe pulled the ball from side to side rapidly and went in for the lay-up.

A Dinsfield player, the center, jumped high with his hand cupped to bat down the ball, but Joe passed off to Castner and Castner's two-handed overhead shot was good.

From such a brilliant start the Tomahawks began to lose their zip as the suspected flu began to take its toll on the boys. Fatigue set in, and the famous Raisner fast break slowed down to a crawl. Speedy Rog Larking was sent to the bench, and Joe Taylor joined him shortly. With the two first string forwards out of the game, Dinsfield showed the edge in speed. They capitalized on it as they realized the Raisner five couldn't run with them anymore.

It was a grueling pace, and the healthy twelve point margin for the Tomahawks began to shrink in the face of Dinsfield's determined rally. Now eight, then six, then four! Raines called a time-out on the last Dinsfield basket.

The boys sopped their faces with the damp towels held out to them while they listened to Raines's terse instructions. Then Raines was directing his instructions to Les.

"Okay, Les, we can't run anymore. Hold up that ball all you can. Watch the bench for my signal, and then keep that ball to stall out the game. If the court gets unbalanced too far, pass off, but don't risk anything, boys, except a clear shot." The coach backed to the bench as they walked unhurriedly out to their positions.

The out of bounds pass went to Larry Ryan. Dinsfield players kept their distance uncertainly, keeping their eyes on Les. Ryan dribbled up the floor cautiously. Now he crossed the ten-second line, still dribbling, but motioning to players with his head. He faked and drew the overanxious players into the corner to cover Joe Taylor. He flipped a pass to Les on the other side of the court.

It was evident to Les that the Dinsfield players respected his shifty tactics, and he was relieved they felt that way about it. If they had only known, he told himself grimly, they could have almost walked up to him in that moment and taken the ball away from him. At least, that was the thought that flashed through his mind.

Les, watching the Dinsfield defense carefully, held the ball up at mid-court and rested it against his hip. Since he hadn't dribbled yet, they still waited for him. He let them wait.

Dinsfield fans arose in their seats and screamed at their players to take the ball away. The players began to advance cautiously, their arms outspread, almost like a dragnet.

Les brought the ball in to his stomach and set his jaw. Just looking into his face must have scared them, because they didn't make any sudden rash moves. Les risked a quick glance at the bench. Jim Raines inclined his head slightly. Les was expected to hold that ball until time ran out on the big clock.

The bounces of the ball were but inches from the floor, controlled by his fingertips. Les remained in place, head up, still watching them as he crouched protectively over the ball.

The dull roar of noise filled the gymnasium, but Les was barely conscious of it now. The roar shrilled into hysterical crescendo as Les eluded the first Dinsfield player and cut around the second one. There wasn't a fan seated now.

The Dinsfield guard threw a body block, but Les leaped over him, not losing a bounce of the ball. Now they were all after him, but he was aware of the comforting presence of crimson uniforms close by.

Two Dinsfield players came from opposite sides

and tried to hem him in between them, but Les dropped back in a deceptive fade just as the more tim-id-hearted Raisner fans began to shriek. He outraced another player and threw a hard chest-level running bounce pass to Johnny Kerr. Johnny stood flat-footed under the basket and angled the ball carefully into the hoop. The substitute forward relieved the tension of the moment by leaping wildly into the air as the gun ended the game. His teammates pounded him on the back as they half-carried him from the floor.

Les was stopped while yet on the playing floor by the Dinsfield captain. The boy held out an out-stretched hand.

"Nice game, Beach."

"Thanks, and the same to you. You guys came on plenty strong."

The boy gave him a last slap on the back and ran across the floor to join his own teammates.

Jim Raines put an arm around Les.

"How do you feel? You had me plenty worried, Les," the coach said. He laughed nervously.

"I could use some rest," Les admitted. Every bone and muscle ached. The sweat inside his bandages had begun to chafe, and he wanted the tape cut away as soon as possible.

Bob Griggs, the basketball talent scout, patted his back as he passed, but Les could manage only a tired grin.

Les eased up on the rubbing table and hunched forward for Doctor Merrill to remove the tape. The scissors slid under the adhesive to part the binding.

Les stepped into the shower room and saw Larry Ryan leaning against the wall, letting the warm water spill over his tired body.

"Boy, am I pooped!" Ryan said with closed eyes.

"You and me both! Hand me the soap, Larry, will you?"

Rip Castner came into the shower room, his eyes showing excitement.

"Hey, you guys heard?"

"Heard what?" Ryan adjusted the water temperature to cool off.

"Both Rog and Joe have the flu all right, but that isn't all."

Larry and Les exchanged an alarmed glance.

"You mean some of the other guys have it too?" Les asked.

"I'll say they do! We only have a five man team to finish the tournament. Three regulars and two second-stringers." Rip's voice rose excitedly as he imparted this discouraging news.

The three boys stared wide-eyed at one another.

"You know what that means," Les said as he reached for his towel. "We've got to play over our heads."

Rip took a quick look at Ryan as he spoke to Les.

"Gee, Les, do you think we can do it? You banged up and all?"

Les faced them, his towel trailing unnoticed to the wet floor.

"Listen, we came into this tournament as a team. We also came into this tournament to win it. I haven't changed my mind on either of those points."

Coach Raines stuck his head through the doorway of the shower room.

"Come on, boys, don't stay in there too long. We want to eat and get all the rest we can."

The boys followed the coach into the main part of the locker room. The players were dressing silently. Their depression was evident at that moment.

Raines smiled bleakly, trying to hide his crashing thoughts, but Les knew the old man must be doing his crying on the inside, where it hurt the most. After years of hopeful anticipation, Jim Raines felt he was going to be thwarted again. This was his last chance. When he spoke to the team, his voice was lifeless.

"We might as well be practical. Get dressed, boys, so we can get out of here."

Les stepped up to the coach's side and faced his teammates.

"Okay, you guys, let's show a little fight! We're not licked yet. Let's nail that sectional for a pretty good guy!"

Once again, Les furnished the spark that fired the Tomahawks. They crowded around the old man. Their whoops and backslaps made Raines duck his head to hide the moisture in his eyes.

"Thanks, boys," Raines muttered huskily as he threw open the door. Each boy's shoulder was gripped warmly as he passed.

CHAPTER TWENTY-SIX

KNUCKLES RATTLED LIGHTLY ON THE HO-tel room door and Larry opened it to admit Doctor Merrill.

The doctor clapped his hat on Larry's head and threw his overcoat over the back of the chair by the small writing table. He put his black satchel beside him as he sat down on the edge of the bed. He crooked his forefinger silently at Larry.

"I'm making a last minute check on you boys for Raines," the doctor explained as he included Rip and Les by looking around Ryan.

His examination of Ryan was quick and efficient. The doctor asked Larry an occasional question, cocking his head until he got an answer. Then he patted the little guard on the rump and turned to Rip, who had edged up to gawk at the proceedings.

"Rip, you're next. How are you feeling?" the doctor asked. He nodded his head as Rip grunted a response to his questions during the examination. Rip received a clean bill of health.

Les stood up from the bed on which he had been lying and began to unbutton his shirt.

"Still all five of us getting to play this afternoon?" he asked.

"Five, if you're okay," the doctor said.

"Well, old All-American is worth half a dozen," Ryan cracked to relieve the suspenseful silence. He and Castner watched almost fearfully as the doctor examined Les.

"He's okay, huh?" Ryan said as Doctor Merrill stood up.

Merrill didn't answer. Instead, he looked into Les's throat and took his pulse.

Les winked as the doctor looked into his eyes. Doctor Merrill grinned and winked back.

"So far, so good. Let's get that tape on you. Hold your arms up a little higher, Les," the doctor said. He rummaged in his bag for the adhesive tape as he spoke. Then he straightened and began to tear off long strips, tacking the ends on the footboard of the bed.

"How do you feel, Les?" the doctor asked conversationally as he continued to tear tape.

"I'm okay now that I've had a good night's sleep and been lying around all morning. Don't worry about me. Sure, I'm a little black and blue in spots, but I'm okay."

The doctor began to place the strips of adhesive tape on Les, pulling them out carefully so they wouldn't wrinkle and turn under.

"Hey, can't you wrap that stuff a little more loosely? The darned tape seems to cut into my armpits," Les said.

"I'll see what I can do, but the idea, Les, is to give you support. You're lucky to be playing at all," the doctor commented.

"That feels better," Les said as he shifted his feet.

"Take a few deep breaths. Hold it. Feel okay? Get your shirt on."

Les picked up his shirt and stuck one arm through the sleeve.

"How are the other boys getting along?"

"Yeah, how about them?" Rip chimed in.

"They're getting sack time, as we used to say in the army. But don't kid yourselves, those boys will be

playing every minute of that game twice over while
they lie there. Of course, they'll be watching the game
on television," Doctor Merrill said. He zipped his
medical bag.

"Television?" Ryan burst out.

"Surely you know the game is being televised. Elmer Robbins, the grocer, and Carl Rice, the appliance
dealer, got together with the hotel management and
rigged the rooms for TV sets."

Ryan struck a pose with a hand on his hip.

"Just think of it, you bums, we're going to be on
TV!"

Doctor Merrill laughed as he opened the door. He
stood in the doorway and looked back at them.

"I see you boys are in better shape than I thought
you were." Then he became more serious. "Just remember to keep those kids in the tournament."

"We intend to," Les said fervently.

"I guess you boys know without my telling you, but
the whole town is pulling for the team. They've never
been this close to a tournament win before. They want
old Jim to get his wish fulfilled. Well, there's not much
I can add except my best wishes. Ralph Watts will
come get you when it's time to report to the gym."

Les moved embarrassedly to the door. Doctor Merrill raised his eyebrows questioningly. Les tried not to
show his lack of ease.

"Doctor Merrill, tell Judy I'll do my best, all the
way."

The doctor winked at him and tapped Les lightly
on the chin.

"Don't be surprised if you hear her yelling over the
rest."

Les turned around to see Rip and Larry standing
with arms intertwined. Les picked up a pillow from
the bed and heaved it at them.

"Okay, lay off."

Rip shook his head.

"Again I say, you lucky guy."

A knock sounded on the door and the boys looked at each other.

"This must be visitor's day," Larry said. He pushed Castner in the direction of the door.

"Hi, Mr. Raines. Come on in." Rip opened the door wider. The Raisner coach entered.

"You boys still have time for a little nap." Suiting action to words, the coach almost tucked them into bed. He adjusted the window shade several times before he was satisfied. He hung over them like a hen with chicks before he tiptoed out of the room.

When the door closed, Rip Castner sat upright in bed. He leaned over and smacked Les on the rump.

"Hey," Les grumbled good-naturedly.

"How in the devil does he expect us to sleep with all that crazy stuff?" Rip said. He wadded up his pillow and placed it higher against the headboard and leaned back against it. He put his leg over the side of the bed and reached his foot across to poke Ryan in the ribs.

Larry propped himself up on his elbow.

"Me, I couldn't go to sleep if I wanted to, which I don't. And I bet Jim Raines won't sleep for two or three nights after this sectional is over."

Les spoke up, but his voice was muffled by the pillow.

"Aw, he means well. The old man is all keyed up. Think of it—twenty years, and no sectional. How would you feel?"

Rip rubbed his head and flopped back to stare up at the ceiling.

"I guess you're right. I suppose I'll coach a million years without winning a sectional."

Ryan winked at Les. He leaned over to Rip.

"Les and I will be papas by that time, Rip boy. We'll send you a little talent."

As Rip sat up to make a retort, Ryan almost bowled him over with a pillow.

Rip pushed the pillow away from his face.

"Sometimes I wonder how I put up with you, Ryan," he said.

"Baloney. Hey, is Les asleep?"

Les was silent. He was thinking too hard. He knew Rip and Larry were trying to relax, trying to be casual, when all the time they were taut as bowstrings. All of them felt the weight of responsibility for their sick teammates, the school and the town. Les tried to put it from his mind. A guy couldn't help it, though.

Guiltily, he thought about himself. What had Bob Griggs, the basketball scout, thought of his playing? Would he get a chance to go to college? Boy, how things worked out! He'd kicked overboard a possible chance when he backed out on Fred Owens. Now another chance might be possible. This time a cleaner way, a better way.

Would he be able to deliver the goods? Would his chest bother him? Now he wished he'd had Doctor Merrill tighten the tape more.

He knew there would be a lot of Raisner people at the game. The Tomahawks had picked up quite a following during the season. More grade school kids hung around the gym. More basketball hoops were beginning to appear on garages in town. Raisner was coming of basketball age.

He'd never be able to fall asleep. What was the use? It wouldn't be long now. How much longer? Yeah, and there was always Billy. Funny how he kept thinking about the kid. Why so much lately? Heck, he'd lived next door to him all his life and hadn't said a dozen words to him.

How would it be not to walk? He tried to think of himself in the same position, but he couldn't. A guy really couldn't, unless it happened to him. You say you understand and, yeah, how tough it is, but you really don't know. Not really.

Funny, too, about that All-American tag the fellows had given him. Probably a joke. Sure, it was a joke. Could he—would he ever be good enough to make All-American in college? Heck, would he ever get to college?

Drowsily, Les was aware of Ryan leaning over him.

"Hey, Rip, Les is asleep, the lucky stiff. I ought to wake him up."

"Aw, Larry, let him alone. You and I both know who's going to pull us through that tournament if anybody does," Rip said.

"Remember how we started out the season, Rip? Everybody hated his guts. I don't know when or how I changed toward Les, or when the other fellows did, for that matter."

"Yeah, I know what you mean. Of course, I've always seen more of him than you other guys did, being as I'm in biology with him every day. You know, Larry, darned if I haven't learned a lot from the cuss," Rip said. He became thoughtfully silent.

"So have I," Ryan admitted.

"I've learned how far a fellow can go if he's got the guts. Take Les. Sure, at first he was kind of sold on himself, but darn it, Larry, he came out of it. You couldn't ask for a better team player than old All-American. You know, just between you and me, I think Les might *be* an All-American someday."

"Heck, I told you that a long time ago."

"Okay, wise guy, I know you did. Larry, we just have to pull this team through the sectional. I'm thinking of Les now."

"What do you mean?"

"So he's a great ballplayer, but who ever hears of great ballplayers unless they win a tournament or two?"

"I see your point. Lots of good players are buried in

the bush leagues. Take that Joe Polinsky, or whatever his name was, you know, the kid that played over at Newton a year or so ago."

"You know, Larry, I never learned what it was to be a competitor until Les came along. Boy, he battles 'em down to the gun. I bet we could be fifty points behind and Les would still be collecting floorburns fighting for that ball."

"We're all better ballplayers because of Les. I don't know how to explain it, but that guy makes me think I can whip my weight in wildcats. I kind of used to feel sorry for myself, being such a runt. Hey, Rip, you fall asleep? Darn you guys, leaving me awake to do all the worrying until game time!"

Les smiled sleepily and dozed off.

Three hours later, Appleton was buzzing with excitement. A five-man Raisner team had downed a game but outclassed Wininger team by a 67 to 49 score. The evening play-off would be Appleton versus Raisner!

The boys, eating in the restaurant after the game, heard comments from Raisner fans, remarks that expressed a fear that they might have burned themselves out in the afternoon game. Of course those statements hadn't been meant for their ears, but they heard them just the same.

Jim Raines sat through the meal, his plate untouched. The stubby fingers drummed incessantly on the tablecloth. His smile was quick and nervous as well-wishers passed the table. He gulped down his cold coffee and pushed back his chair as the boys finished their meals.

Les wondered what thoughts were going through the coach's mind. Twenty years was a long time to wait. Twenty years, but these last few hours were the most difficult of all!

CHAPTER TWENTY-SEVEN

THE WAIT, THE STRAIN OF THE PRE-GAME wait, seemed almost endless, yet before they realized it the boys were staring at each other in the locker room. The new red satin warm-up jackets were bright under the light.

This was it! They scuffed their shoes against the floor and chewed vigorously on their gum.

Raines, who had probably rehearsed a hundred fight talks for such an opportunity as a final sectional game, sat speechless, staring down at the floor. From time to time he would look at the boys, seemingly about to say something. Instead, he would lick his lips and glance at his wrist watch. Les, watching the old man closely, saw him wind his watch three different times. Finally the coach lurched to his feet and faced the team.

"We got past Wininger without anyone getting into serious trouble on personal fouls. That's going to be harder to do this evening. Boys, you have to watch your step. I'll tell you what to do from the bench, but when you're on the floor, Les is the boss. You follow his instructions, because he will be following mine. Got it?"

For an answer, Ryan slipped up behind Les and gave him a Dutch rub.

"Hey!" Les yelled good-naturedly, ducking another attempt.

Raines pressed his lips but said nothing. The horse-play at a time like this upset him.

Ralph Watts came into the dressing room, his eyes snapping with excitement.

"Time!"

Again the coach and his players exchanged those quick glances. Then their eyes held. They drew together into a tight knot.

"Go take 'em, gang!" Raines said.

The boys burst from the dressing room, eager to get on the floor and loosen up. The coach looked at his wrist watch again as he walked more slowly behind them.

Les and the team stopped abruptly before going on the floor. Bob Sage had moved to the center circle and the gym hushed.

"What's going on?" Ryan whispered uncertainly.

"I don't know." Rip Castner pushed in between Larry and Les.

Then the announcer's voice on the public address system enlightened them.

"Bob Sage, of Appleton, is going to sink three baskets from center court."

Sage bounced the ball and grinned crookedly at the Raisner team standing at the side line. His first shot snipped through the net without touching the hoop. Clinton, the Appleton center, returned the ball to him.

When Sage's second shot duplicated the first, Les looked at his teammates. He saw the worry, the anxiety, the growing uncertainty. It bothered him.

The crowd's roar ended the demonstration as Bob Sage made his third straight shot from the center circle. Appleton fans were jubilant. Raisner fans tried to yell them down, but Les could feel the fear in their voices.

Rip grabbed Les by the arm.

"Les, you have to do something. This cold war is

giving the guys the willies. You can do anything Sage can do. Go ahead."

"You think I'm nuts, or something? You know what everyone has ridden me about before. It would look like I was grandstanding. Anyway, maybe I couldn't do it," Les answered, but a speculative gleam was in his eye.

Appleton fans laughed from across the floor as their cheer leaders gave them instructions for a yell. Then the yell came at them full force.

"We want Beach! We want Beach!"

A dozen Raisner football lettermen sitting together cupped their hands to their mouths and yelled back at them.

"You'll wish you had him before this game is over!"

Les looked at the two second-stringers with them for this game tonight. Johnny Kerr and Bob Gray shifted their eyes away from him. Les set his jaw. These guys were scared. They needed a boost. He held out both hands to Johnny Kerr.

"Give me the ball, Johnny."

The Raisner fans yelled as Les bounced the ball experimentally while he walked out to the center of the floor. The silence hit Les then like a blow.

He looked to the bench. Jim Raines sat there as though petrified. Then he realized why Les was going to shoot. He slapped his hands together, and Les saw his lips move, "Good luck, Les!"

Appleton fans jeered as Les came back off the floor. They thought he wasn't going to shoot. The words of the announcer cast a tenseness over the gym that was electric. Even Jim Raines looked startled.

"Beach of Raisner says he will not shoot from the center circle only. He will move clockwise around the court at the center stripe. Get this, folks, Beach says he will sink ten consecutive baskets!"

Rip Castner moved out to Les in that moment and put his mouth close to Les's ear.

"Atta baby, Les boy. You can do it."

Les nodded a brief thanks and moved out to the floor. Then he was alone on that big floor, the Appleton team having moved off.

Of all the foolish stunts! Les condemned himself in a strained whisper. Why had he brought all this on himself? A morale booster! Yeah, all he had to do was to miss one shot and be hooted off the floor. Then what would happen to those guys who had begged him with their eyes to better Bob Sage? Why hadn't he said four baskets, or five at the most?

Thoughts flashed through his mind as though running through a movie projector. "We are troubled on every side, yet not distressed; we are perplexed, but not in despair; persecuted, but not forsaken; cast down, but not destroyed!"

Hope flamed through Les. This was to be his night! He knew it now without a shadow of a doubt. A grin spread across his face. He faced the backboard unafraid.

"One!" was counted by five thousand throats.

Les dribbled the ball behind him as he walked to his next position, and the Tomahawk war whoop rang through the gym.

Les sighted, dipped his knees and sent the ball arching high into the air. Too high! No, it plunked pleasingly into the hoop.

"Two!"

"Three!"

"Four!"

"Five!"

The sixth shot trembled on the hoop and then, as breath was released explosively throughout the gym, the ball fell through the net.

"Seven!" Les thought he could hear Rip Castner's voice bellowing out louder than anyone else.

Les steadied himself. The tape tugged at his arm-

204   JOHN F. CARSON

pits. He stood there for a moment, holding the ball in his hands.

"Eight!"

"Nine!"

Now Les was on the far side of the court, nearest to the Raisner cheering section. He wiped his hand on his trunks as the ball bounced in front of him in a lazy high bounce.

The front row spectators seemed but an arm's length away. Les tried not to be distracted by their well-meant encouragement. Then he heard a voice surprisingly distinct for its softness.

"You can do it, Les!"

He turned his head then. Judy was leaning forward. Her face was radiant with pride. Les turned his head away quickly, his emotions almost overpowering him in that suspenseful moment. His fingers trembled as they gripped the ball. He felt the grain of the leather pressing into them.

Should he try to angle the ball into the hoop, taking advantage of the backboard? No, he finally decided. He always shot for the hoop. He wouldn't change now.

Even as Les readied himself for the final attempt, he marveled at the good sportsmanship displayed by the Appleton fans. No one tried to heckle him. They waited in respectful silence, a tribute to a great basketball player.

"Ten!"

Les thought he was going to sag to the floor he was so relieved. Joyous screams from Tomahawks fans followed him to the players' bench. Alarmed speculation began to make itself audible from the Appleton side of the floor.

Fans from both teams applauded as Bob Sage came to the Raisner bench to shake Les's hand.

"Nice going, you crazy nut!" But Sage was grinning

as he said it. Les felt a friendly attraction toward the
other player.

"I would have hated to try another shot," Les admitted as he returned Sage's handclasp.

The Tomahawks were burning with a new fire now.
They cut ball handling capers they probably wouldn't
be able to duplicate the next day.

"Les, you crazy, wonderful guy!" Rip hugged him
gleefully.

"Ouch! Hey, lay off, Rip."

Castner stepped back, sudden concern on his face.

"Gee, I'm sorry. I forgot, Les. How are you feeling?"

"After the luck I just had, you should ask," Les said.

"Les, it was great! That's a shooting demonstration I
never expect to see duplicated under the same pressure."

"I just hope I didn't run out of baskets," Les answered. He saw Raines motioning to him and he went
to the bench for what he knew were to be his game instructions as the playmaker of the squad.

"Les, I'm glad I didn't have the sense to stop you.
Nothing I could ever have said would have bucked up
the boys the way you just did. That's why you did it,
wasn't it?"

Les nodded his head. Again he thought about the
ironic twist of events. Now his shooting ability had
been put to a good cause, a team cause, and it hadn't
netted a single point. But the results were likely to
yield an overall scoring total that would surpass any
he might make as an individual.

"They're pretty good guys," was all Les said.

Then Raines got down to business. Oh, he had gone
over these plays several times with Les, twice in the
coach's home, in fact, but Raines reviewed the high-
lights in a fast, tight-clipped voice.

Les rejoined his teammates in their pre-game warm-
up. With only five of them on the floor, the ball

whipped around rapidly. Les stationed himself under the boards and passed out from the lay-ups as each player cut in his turn. He kept a stream of encouraging banter going as each player came down from his leap. They ran back to their places to smack the teammate ahead of them on the tail, seemingly spurring him to greater effort.

Then the big gym once again hushed into silence. The players on the floor put the basketballs down and faced the big flag.

The national anthem had never sounded better to Les. Friend and foe alike chorused the words, the words that bound them together.

After the last note had trailed away, the boys left the floor and went down into the locker room for what could be the last time of the basketball season.

This time Jim Raines was ready. He was flushed with newborn hope and enthusiasm. He allowed no one in these pre-game sessions, and there were no distractions. The coach grinned tensely.

"Boys, they're scared out of their shoes. Let's keep 'em that way. We're undermanned. It calls for all the team play you can use. You won't get much rest. They'll try to run you off your feet. You'll get tired, maybe a gut ache or two. You'll have to dig in and play on heart. You've got that heart! That's the stuff champions are made of!" Raines's eyes snapped with excitement.

"Be careful on those fouls, but don't let it freeze you. Play as you always have, but remember, it's not just another game. It's a sectional championship! It's our ticket to the regional tournament." The varsity coach looked searchingly into each boy's eyes. They saw the hopes shining in his. Optimism fired those hopes. That was enough for them.

"Let's get 'em, what do you say, you guys!" Rip Castner leaped to his feet, poised to bolt through the door. Others crowded on his heels.

"Let's go! Let's go!" Ryan yelled. His voice was strained by the excitement.

Les drew a deep experimental breath against the tape. Everything seemed all right, but he wished he didn't have to wear it.

Raines threw open the door and four members of the team shot out like greyhounds. Les turned to Raines. The coach and his protégé gripped hands.

"I'm counting on you, Les. Don't let them lose their heads when they get excited. It's been a long road, Les. I'm glad we're taking it together."

"This one is for you," Les said. Then he ran after his teammates.

CHAPTER TWENTY-EIGHT

"GO GET 'EM, BIG TEAM! GO GET 'EM!" RAIS-
ner fans were on their feet when the Tomahawks
took the floor.

The ball shone under the lights as it left the official's
hands. The sectional final was on!

Clinton, the Appleton center, took the tip, but Les
was there to get it. He brought the ball down the side
line.

"Shoot! Shoot!" Raisner fans begged. It was a
different kind of yelling than Les had faced during the
first game of the season. This time, however, he was
barely conscious of it. He was concentrating on setting
up the play. From the corner of his eye he caught a
glimpse of Johnny Kerr cutting for the backboard. His
strong-wristed pass bounced a step ahead of Kerr,
leading him to the basket. Johnny took it without
breaking his speed and went into the air to score the
first two points of the game.

Due to the shortage of manpower, the Tomahawks
quickly went to their zone formation without attempting their usual press.

Les shifted and then went in to the board as he saw
Horst of Appleton come in from the other side. His
fingers snatched the ball from the backboard a frac-
tion of a second before Clinton was able to capture
the rebound.

Les twisted and dodged, driving the ball from his

left to his right hand as he wove through the melee. Now only Bob Sage of the Tigers was between him and the basket down court. Les sidestepped, faked a hand change and sped his dribble. Sage tried to shift with him, but Les was too fast.

Bob Gray yelled at Les from across court, and Les leaped up beyond Sage's outflung arms and hooked a pass to the substitute forward. Bob juggled the ball as he ran, and the referee called traveling.

"That's okay, Bob!" Les said encouragingly. Then Les set himself for the center court pass-in play Appleton tried to put into immediate operation. He pointed toward the defensive basket to Ryan as the ball handler got around Johnny Kerr. Ryan tied it up for a jump ball.

Larry stepped back from the referee and waited until he was sure his teammates were in position. Then he crouched for the jump.

The Tigers controlled the tip and the ball went back to sharpshooting Bob Sage. Les crowded him for a hurried shot. Castner took the rebound. Out to Kerr. Kerr over to Gray. Back to Castner, then the ball was sidearmed to Ryan. The Tigers went down to set up their defense.

Les took Larry's pass, then returned it. He stood in front of Ryan and the little guard sank a nice long one. Score, Raisner 4, Appleton 0.

Appleton scored. Les brought the ball up court. Sage, his face determined, moved cautiously in front of Les. Les straightened and flipped a pass over to Ryan. From Larry, the ball went into the corner. Gray tried a one-hander. The ball bounced on the hoop.

Les batted the ball into the net on his rebound. Again the scoreboard changed. Raisner 6, Appleton 2.

Appleton called time out. Play was resumed. Bob Sage, who had been effectively bottled up by Les, shifted to a forward position. Appleton needed his scoring punch. Johnny Kerr was no match for the elusive Sage. Sage's efforts brought the Tigers from the trailing score to a tie.

Kerr picked up two personal fouls as he tried to stop Sage. The Tiger guard made both counters good. Appleton went into the lead.

On the only rebound he was to get in the game, McIntosh tipped in another two points. Clinton made a nice pivot shot over Rip's head. An Appleton rally began to unfold with terrifying quickness.

As Les brought the ball down court he glanced at the clock. The first quarter lacked but two minutes of being over. Appleton now led, 12 to 6.

Les passed to Ryan. Larry brought the ball along the center stripe and handed it to him. Les faked and cut around him. He drove for the backboard, stopped abruptly and went into the air for a two-handed jump shot. The ball rocketed through the hoop.

Bob Gray made body contact with Horst on the pass-in. Horst sank the foul. Anxious to redeem himself, Bob tried to pull a ball steal from Clinton, and the Tiger center toed the foul stripe. His shot was good. Again the Appleton team held its six point advantage.

Les opened up from far out on the court and sank two baskets before the quarter came to an end. Score, Appleton 14, Raisner 12!

Ralph Watts threw towels to them as they came to the bench. Raines cautioned Kerr and Gray about fouls. It had been a game remarkably free of fouling by either team, and the spectators were enjoying a game unmarred by too frequent whistle blowing.

The Appleton Tigers, after a comparatively slow start for them, began to hit the stride that had caused them to drop only two seasonal games in their schedule. The powerful host team began to find the range more often.

Under Raines's instructions, the ball was fed back to Les, and he took over the Tomahawk offense. It was disheartening to Raisner fans when Les, after a brilliant .750 clip, and scoring sixteen points in that quarter, failed to close the gap between the two teams. Appleton continued to lead, 33 to 28 when the second quarter ended.

Equally disappointing was the fact Johnny Kerr now had four personal fouls!

The boys were breathing heavily when they entered the locker room. Raines let them relax before he made any comments.

"You've done a great job, boys. A great job. The only trouble is, you're going to have to do a better one if you're going to win it." The coach turned to Johnny Kerr. The substitute forward was sobbing his disappointment in himself.

"Buck up, Johnny," Raines said in a kindly tone. "You're doing your best, and that's all any coach can expect from a player. We can't afford to lose you. Try to watch it."

Les motioned to Doctor Merrill, who had entered the room quietly.

"Snip some of that tape from under my right arm, will you?"

"Holding up okay?" The doctor tried to keep his voice casual.

Les shot a quick look at him.

"Sure, sure. I'm all right."

"You're playing a whale of a game, Les. It's your best by far," the doctor whispered to him as he cut away the tape.

"It's not good enough." Les couldn't keep the frustration from his voice. He so much wanted the team to win!

Les became aware of the coach's instructions. He concentrated on those words.

"Les, we need you under the backboard for both offense and defense now. It's going to run you ragged. We have to stop Sage!" Raines smacked his fist into his hand.

The play during that third quarter can still raise a good conversation around drugstore counters.

Les held the sharpshooting Tiger guard scoreless! Meanwhile, Les sank three baskets. In turn, he set up Ryan to take over the bulk of the Tomahawk offense. Little Larry came through, in spite of the defensive height he had to shoot over.

Raisner yells pierced the air when the hard-fighting Tomahawks crept into a tie, and then began to open the gap. Their joy was short-lived when Johnny Kerr picked up his fifth personal foul with but twenty seconds remaining of the third quarter. The scoreboard now showed: Raisner 47, Appleton 43.

Only four Tomahawks remained in the game, carrying the hopes of their absentee teammates, coach and home town on their weary shoulders. Raines blew his nose vigorously. Les knew he was wondering how only four players could be a match for a hard-hitting team like Appleton. Les found himself wondering the same thing.

The Raisner team was startled to see George Crandell, the Appleton coach take time during the intermission to speak to Raines.

"You've got a great bunch of boys, Jim. I know how much this tournament means to you."

"You bet they're a great bunch of boys. But the game isn't over yet. Listen to that, if you don't believe me." The old coach faced the crimson and white cheering section.

"WE'VE GOT A TEAM, NOBODY PROUDER, AND IF YOU CAN'T HEAR US, WE'LL YELL A LITTLE LOUDER! BEAT APPLETON! BEAT APPLETON! GO, TEAM, GO!"

Crandell listened silently, then he grinned.

"You always were a sentimental cuss, Jim. I think that's why I like you. Let the best team win, but I can't help wishing you a little luck."

"Better save some of that luck for yourself," Raines flung after him.

CHAPTER TWENTY-NINE

THE FOUR TOMAHAWKS GRINNED AS THEY
listened to the Raisner yells. They were making a
last swipe of the towels across their faces when another yell made them pause to look at each other.

"WILL WE, CAN WE, YES, YES, YES, WIN THIS
GAME FOR R. H. S.!"

Jim Raines found it somewhat easier to grab four
pairs of hands than the usual five.

"You heard them, gang! They're with you, all the
way!"

The fourth quarter began in a flurry of fast action
that caused the ball to alternate between the Appleton
team and the Raisner team in rapid succession.

The sports announcer was having a verbal fit on the
microphone. His listeners were thoroughly sold that
this was the most important sectional championship
being played in the state that night. If they thought
the name of Beach was familiar to them, they were to
find it would be more so.

Les knew the Tomahawks had to protect that lead
or Appleton would close them out in a stall. But with
only four men on the Raisner team would Appleton
even have to stall? Heck, they'd probably shower
them with points.

Les dribbled in place while he sized up the
offensive court. Rip, Gray and Ryan were dodging
crazily among the Appleton defense—faking, faking,
faking—but they were wasting energy. The Tigers

had them under control. Then Sage and Horst came out to get Les.

Les watched the two guards warily. He crouched lower over the ball, his head up. Two on one, that was the way it would be! Appleton had a spare man to help guard Les, and they were taking advantage of it.

Les didn't want to get trapped into a charging penalty, so he began to move the ball away from the tantalizing opening between the Tiger guards. He had almost taken the chance, but with three personal fouls on him he didn't dare risk it.

Sage moved slowly over until he was now standing several feet in front of Les, while Horst moved up to edge him toward the side line. Les didn't want to get boxed in between the center stripe and the side line. He reversed himself and cut past Horst.

Bob Sage shifted with him, but Les was determined it would take a truck to stop him now. Les spun in place, almost going down, recovered and headed for the backboard.

Clinton and McIntosh were anchored in front of the board. Les headed for them and went up into the air. Their arms formed a barrier over his head, and Les hooked the ball behind him to Larry Ryan. Larry used the advantage of the off-balance Appleton height and pegged a two-handed jump shot into the hoop. Score, Raisner 49, Appleton 43!

Appleton brought the ball down court fast. Raisner players backpedaled fearfully, afraid they had allowed the offense to get behind them.

Castner was neatly blocked and Les was forced to wait out a possible rebound.

Les almost went up too soon. The ball circled the hoop twice and came out into his ready hands. (The radio announcer claimed that Les was four feet off the floor.) Twisting in midair, Les passed the ball to the waiting Ryan. Larry was clear! Les fell backward and was aware of a sharp pain stabbing through his body.

He put out his hands to break his fall and from a dazed sitting position he watched little Ryan make his lay-up good.

Rip bent over Les anxiously.

"Les, you okay?"

Horst was coming down court with the ball. Les yelled at Rip to take the Tiger guard and got to his feet. Horst scissored into the air and made the field goal.

Raines called time. Les saw the coach watching him closely as he came to the bench.

"Les, sit down."

The coach nibbled at his lip as he gave the command.

Les looked at Raines.

"We can't play with three men!"

Raines had involuntarily glanced at the bench for a replacement for Les, forgetting in the excitement that there were no replacements.

"I'm okay. I'm okay!" Les said fiercely, but he knew he shouldn't play. He put an arm over Castner and Ryan and hung his head while breathing deeply. The pain subsided. He nodded his head to show that he was listening as Raines gave instructions to the other three players.

"Slow down the game as much as you can when you have the ball. It will cut down on our scoring chances, but we have to have a breather."

Les looked at the clock. Five minutes remained of the game.

Sixty seconds later Appleton had scored two baskets, bringing the team total to 47, one basket away.

Thirty seconds passed, and Appleton went into the lead. Sage had made a lay-up and a foul which had been called on Bob Gray. Score, Appleton 50, Raisner 49!

Les took the ball out of bounds. Were the Tomahawks to be thwarted in these last few minutes? The game four-man team had played all out, but it hadn't been enough. Now was no time to get fainthearted.

Les gritted his teeth as the Appleton victory chant welled like a giant's pulsebeat across the playing floor. How long had he been holding the ball out of bounds looking for a pass receiver?

Ryan made the barest sign with his head, but Les had been watching for it. Les bent down and rolled the ball across the floor, leading Larry by several feet to the side, but to his relief Ryan got it on the dead run. But it brought Larry too deeply into the corner of the court.

Larry tried to pass, but the ball hit against Horst's arm, and began to bounce crazily as eager hands reached for it. The ball seemed to spurt from fingers as they attempted to close around it.

Finally, Rip Castner reached down and batted it down court. The flight of the ball straightened as it skimmed over the floor. Past the keyhole, across the center stripe, almost to the offensive foul circle! Les scooped it up as the ball cut across the foul lane. He teetered for balance, regained it, took a step out and sank a left-handed push shot.

The Appleton victory chant ended with a startled squawk! Once more the four-man team was in the lead, but by a bare one-point margin, 51 to 50.

Two minutes and fifty-three seconds remained of the game as Bob Sage brought the ball down court from the pass-in. Then Les was in front of him, weaving with the ball handler.

Sage made one mistake, his only one of the game, when he tried to outmaneuver Les. Les shot his hand in and took Sage's dribble away from him, not losing a bounce.

Raisner fans screamed hysterically as Les sidestepped to keep from getting caught by the awakened Tiger defense. Horst and Sage descended upon him, and Les's shoes screeched as he changed direction.

Les fell to one knee, and the hot bite of the floorburn caused him to grimace. Sage leaped wildly over him to avoid fouling. Les found himself wishing he had been fouled. Then he was moving forward again. He couldn't stand still, not now!

Les was afraid to take his eyes from the opposition, yet he wanted to find his own teammates. The sudden deadliness of the hush that descended then made him wonder how much time remained. Already it seemed as though an hour had passed.

Now Les knew how a fox must feel when the hounds are closing in for the kill. This time they were Tigers. Perspiration coursed down his face and he blinked rapidly, trying to clear his eyes. The sweat stung. He wanted to brush it away. He didn't dare!

Two, three, four, how many players were after him? Les dodged. It was like a nightmare. Hands, hands, hands.

A voice came to him. It was Castner.

"Forty-five seconds, Les. Forty-five seconds!"

Les tried to place Rip by his voice, but he couldn't. Now his chest ached again. He wanted to straighten up. Where was everybody? The sweat smarted in his eyes as he shook his head. Then someone was blocking his path. Les brought the ball in to his body to protect it. Something hit him in the knees and he fell. Hands wrenched at the ball, twisting savagely, but his fingers dug deeper into the pebbled grain.

A whistle shrilled almost in his ears. As Les got to his feet, he pulled out the tail of his jersey and wiped his eyes. Automatically, his eyes went up to the clock. Three seconds!

But the whistle! What about the whistle?

"Two shots, Beach."

The referee tucked the ball under his arm and trotted to the foul stripe.

"Sink 'em, Les baby!" Larry Ryan yelled with his hand cupped to his mouth.

"Put 'er in, Les," Bob Gray said as he took his position under the backboard. His arms were half-raised to shield the rebound.

Rip Castner came up behind Les as he took the ball from the referee and stepped away from the stripe.

"Okay, All-American, you can do it!"

Les looked at Rip and grinned as the lanky center winked back at him. He bounced the ball and stepped up to toe the stripe.

The basket seemed so far away. Les felt his knees catch as he dipped for the shot. Now the ball was arching into the air. His eyes and five thousand other pairs of eyes watched the ball hang for a moment in the air and then gracefully drop through the net.

Again Les stepped back from the foul stripe. He wiped his hands on his trunks. The official handed the ball to him and nodded his head.

The net squeezed the ball and then let it drop through. Both foul shots had been good! Score, Raisner 53, Appleton 50.

The Tomahawks moved slowly after the fast-breaking Tiger five. They had no intention of committing a foul. The Appleton shot was good. Score, Raisner 53, Appleton 52! There were some who later questioned whether the last Appleton basket actually counted. They claimed time had run out. It no longer mattered. Jim Raines had won his first sectional tournament.

As Les walked toward the tunnel entrance he sucked in his breath sharply. It was over. Thank goodness, it was over! The tape had worked itself loose, but he didn't care. It was over!

Rip threw his warm-up jacket over his shoulders as he walked.

"How do you feel, Les?"

Les saw the deep eyes watching his anxiously.

"Tired," Les cracked.

"Boy, if I live to be a hundred, Les, I never expect

to see ball handling like that again. They were all after you, Les. The whole darned Appleton team
couldn't take the ball away from you without fouling
you." Rip's voice rang with as much pride as though
he had done the feat himself.

Larry Ryan ran up and turned Rip and Les around.

"Hey, you guys, come back here. We're going to cut
the net down."

The ladder had already been placed under the west
hoop.

Someone, Les thought it was Ralph Watts but there
was so much happy confusion he didn't know, slipped
a jackknife into his hand. But Les stepped back with a
grin. He winked at his teammates.

"How about it, fellows?"

They knew what he meant. They pushed Jim Raines
up to the ladder. Silently, Les handed the knife to the
coach. Tears were running down the man's face, making a comical sight as they ran down the deep creases
of his grin.

"Help me up the ladder, fellows, I can't see a
blamed thing without my glasses," Raines said. Willing hands helped him up.

"Go ahead, coach, whack 'er down! The next one is
ours!" Larry Ryan yelled.

Raines sawed vigorously. No net could have with-
stood the assault that had been ripening for twenty
years.

The Raisner fans yelled as each player took his turn
on the ladder under the east basket. Les, as acting
captain, had modestly declined until last. No one had
to beg peppery little Ryan to go up the ladder first.

From Larry, the knife went to Rip Castner. Rip cut
generously before he surrendered the blade to Bob
Gray. Two strands remained when Les got the knife.

When Les started up the ladder the gym seemed to
explode with the huge ovation. Les looked out at the
sea of faces. This was for him!

"We are troubled on every side, yet not distressed; we are perplexed, but not in despair; persecuted, but not forsaken; cast down, but not destroyed!"

It wasn't perspiration now that made him blink his eyes. He thought about the people who had helped him along the way. As he reached to cut the remaining strands, a flashbulb popped almost in his face. He was to keep that picture. It showed a different Les Beach, a face of humility.

Familiar faces hemmed the hardwood as the boys and their coach walked to the tunnel. Les saw Miss Garr and Miss Wheeler dabbing their eyes with those dinky handkerchiefs women carried, but they were laughing like schoolgirls. Yes, that tall man whose balding head was above those around him, that was Reverend Maynard. Elmer Robbins' laughing eyes were almost hidden in his round cheeks. And there was Judy!

Les slowed down. Judy strained against the surging crowd, waving frantically for him to see her. Then she stood next to him. Her upturned face was very close to his. Les felt a sudden impulse to kiss her, but people around them guessed his intention and laughed. Instead he winked boyishly, which brought scarlet tints to Judy's cheeks. The moment was lost. He was pushed toward the tunnel by well-meaning people.

His dad threw an affectionate arm around him. Les winced, but didn't say anything. His dad couldn't talk anyway.

Doctor Merrill had been unwinding tape, anticipating his coming. The doctor stopped and gripped Les's hand warmly.

"Les, you're a champion."

Judy's father stepped away as Jim Raines moved forward.

The chatter in the locker room quieted as the coach and his protégé shook hands.

"Les, all of us are mighty, mighty proud of you.

Peel that jersey. I want that big number eleven hanging in our school trophy case as a reminder to other
boys how tough a team-playing competitor can be!"

Les looked at the coach with unwavering eyes.

"Maybe they can remember, too, that basketball is
more than a game!" Les said huskily.

The Tomahawks drew together and put their arms
around each other. Then Larry Ryan let out a yip.

"Watch out, you big lug, you stepped on my foot!"

The sentimental setting was broken. Together, the
boys dragged a struggling and protesting Larry Ryan
into the shower stall and turned the water on him.

"Go get 'em, big team!" Larry gasped happily.